PRAISE FOR LINDSAY LERMAN

"A beautiful treatise on grief and everything that comes after—the uncertain friendships, the numbness, the regret, and, eventually, the newer, different life. For everyone that's ever grappled with an ending, only to discover something new and beautiful about themselves, this is a touching debut that evokes elements of both Leonard Cohen's The Favorite Game and Max Porter's Grief is the Thing with Feathers."

"Devastating insight into feminine consciousness unbound."

"Breathtakingly honest, intimate, sexy, and sad, this book is the soft, subversive voice whispering wisdom in the eye of the global hurricane. I love it immensely. And if you still have a sputtering spark in your soul, you probably will too."

"Lindsay Lerman's "I'm From Nowhere" rages with the quiet intensity of a lake concealing an inferno. It's the kind of book where you have to put your ear really close up to it in order to hear the screaming inside. A woman's husband is dead, and her male friends hover nearby like vultures in the aftermath. It reminds me in a lot of ways of C.S Lewis' 'A Grief Observed.' in that there are no easy answers.

There aren't even any easy questions.

Just a woman in pain trying to pick up the pieces of a life shattered, and wondering if she even had a life to begin with. I can't help but feel this book took a piece of me with it. Insinuated itself into me, and lingered like an echo in an empty space."

I'M FROM NOWHERE

LINDSAY LERMAN

CL◀SH

Copyright © 2019 by Lindsay Lerman

Cover by Matthew Revert

matthewrevertdesign.com

Author bio pic by Sandy Swagger Jones

CLASH Books

clashbooks.com

This is for you.

Go with me.

"I should like to be the landscape which I am contemplating, I should like this sky, this quiet water to think themselves within me, that it might be I whom they express in flesh and bone, and I remain at a distance."

SIMONE DE BEAUVOIR, *THE ETHICS OF AMBIGUITY*

ONE

The day of the funeral arrives.

Claire has known this day was coming for at least the past few days, but now she feels unable to face it. All those hands in need of shaking, all those faces in need of acknowledging, the endless hugs she'll have to give and receive. Why this injunction to publicly grieve? Must she prove to the world that she loved John? That she is crippled by his death? She is crippled by his death.

This funeral is for them, not for her. Her funeral for John has been a continuous one. Puking in the toilet, clutching the little packet of tissues in her hand, wiping her mouth and wishing there were no mirror above the sink--wishing she didn't have to see her terrible face.

This morning she is watching from the window as a dog runs wildly down the street in front of their house. A leash-less dog, going from nowhere to nowhere. Should she go outside, see if the dog will slow down for her? Will the dog dart in front of a speeding car? Will she have to watch the dog wriggle and howl in pain as it dies? Will she comfort it? *Did someone see John in his last moments?* she wonders.

Did someone have to watch him howl and grab at the air and gulp in his last hopeful breaths? Did that someone comfort him, usher him out? She has been conducting a private funeral since the moment of the call—a funeral with blurry borders, the grieving spilling into the puking, the clutching, the watching. She would prefer to keep doing it this way. She wants to remain in her bed, her pajamas, her air-conditioned bedroom glowing with sunlight, where she can puke on her own terms.

She is spending too much time figuring out what to wear, how to put herself together. Should she be unkempt? Or coiffed, as though a best friend or a sister had been here to do her makeup and hair? She is alone. There is no one here today to dress her or even make her a cup of coffee. She holds a black dress, probably a gift from John, that she hasn't worn in years. Is it a beautiful dress? Should she wear a beautiful dress? How *does* one perform the depth of one's sadness?

She cares more about what everyone—what *they*—will think of her than she'd like to admit. Will they think this lipstick looks too celebratory? Will they cluck their tongues if she does what she wants to, and instead arrives in these worn-out flannel pants missing their drawstring and this shirt with yellowing sweat stains? Will they see in her eyes that she doesn't know if she can face them? But the important thing is to try, isn't it? *Try*.

She will drive herself to the ceremony, in this not-too-short black dress, as the heat of the morning tries to break into the car to rob her of her moisture. The monsoons are almost here, but not yet. The heat reminds her—urges her—to go back inside. It punishes her for staying outside. The sun never seems to go down.

The dog is still in the street, but it is motionless now, watching her climb into the car, watching her struggle to be as still as possible until the air conditioning starts working and she can put her face in the way of one little stream of cool air.

What had he said the other morning, as he left? she wonders. *Let's have steaks for dinner?* The luxury of it seems entirely impossible to her now.

She remembers once telling him, *I want you to undo me. I want you to take me apart.* And he had.

In his death, he was doing it again.

TWO

She sits flanked by his loving parents. Her in-laws. An honest, kind, hard-working couple, in love with the safe, calm life they had built for themselves over the years. In love with their now-dead son, their only child. An attentive, beautiful boy who grew into an attentive, handsome husband. As with mother and father, so with wife.

She sits in this room. A room crowded with people, cards, flowers, photos, packages, all small or large tokens. All sad manifestations of solidarity, understanding, condolence. That terrible word that just rolls around the mouth: *condolences*.

It's true that people are thinking of her, hoping she will be well. They give their love to her because they can no longer give it to John. And yes, it's true that their offerings of affection and concern are better than nothing— better than silence. Or are they? What can their concern *do*? What would happen if she knocked over the vases, tore up the cards, sat down in the middle of the room and just looked at everyone? *Am I pathetic to them?* she wonders.

John's mother holds Claire's hand, sandwiched between her two smooth, sweaty hands. His mother looks at her, looks right in her eyes, and Claire can't help it—they are crying together, trading strangled sobs. Claire had hoped to not do this, not yet. Not in front of everyone, not here.

His father is often emotive, but now he sits quietly, hands folded tightly in his lap, his shoulders pulled slightly forward. Claire looks at him and can't figure out what he's thinking. Is he planning something? A future trip? Or wondering something. Were John's finances secure? Will Claire be alright? What will happen next? With his shoulders like that, he looks so small. *I don't like seeing him look weak,* she thinks.

Andrew and Luke are seated in the back of the room, near the door. From time to time, Claire notices them whispering to each other. She hasn't seen the two of them in the same room in 4 years? 5 years? She has seen Andrew regularly for the past few years—since she and John moved here—but it's been a lifetime since they've all been together. They are happy to be near each other, she can tell. But they are all too aware of the circumstances under which they've been reunited, so it's not quite excitement they're expressing.

———

Everyone is wearing black, no one looks healthy or robust. The sunlight floods the room, the room feels stuffy. *Why are we in a church?* she wonders. *John was never religious.* Here is a cluster of friends, there is a cluster of more distant family members.

John was loved. It is clear. One by one, friends and coworkers and family members tiptoe up to the podium to deliver their touching and appropriately funny stories of John's charming youthful foolishness and his wise-beyond-his-years dependability. A perfect combination, really.

A cousin named Elizabeth remembers one night in college when she came to visit John, and they went out and drank too much and had to stumble home to John's apartment. But Elizabeth lost one of her dried-out contacts on the way and threatened to give up, to sleep on the curb for the night. John the gentleman did his drunken best to carry Elizabeth piggyback all the way home, though he'd been even drunker and his legs were getting sore.

The solemn room gets the release of laughter. *They* get to chuckle as they wipe away their tears; they get to remember, in so doing, that they will be okay. Claire has no such luxury this morning. There is no release, no soothing comfort of the release. *They* will never suffer with her.

What would happen if she threw the boxes of chocolates into the aisles, if she broke the bottles of wine on the tops of the pews? What would happen if she stood up and tore her clothes off and shouted *Look at me?* Why can't she hand her suffering off to these people? *They want to help, don't they?*

The stories keep coming. John made such a good cup of coffee. John took care of his friends. Even as a child, John didn't smash his playmates' castles or cities or houses made of blocks. John had the loudest laugh. John wanted one day to be a good father. John was exceptional. From the moment he was born to the moment he died, most people he met were impressed.

Most of these stories are known to her. She watches with sadness as she sees that most of them are new to her in-laws. *Had they known him?* she wonders. They had always wanted to know him—they had taken interest in him. But she can see that like her, they are struggling to listen well. They have the selective memories and attention spans of the grieving. How is it, she wonders, that so much mental energy can be consumed by what she can only call numbness?

There are moments when it subsides and she finds herself present enough to control her crying, to make it less ugly, with less snot dripping from her nose. There's no point, though, she realizes, because as soon as she gains control of the numbness, she can hear all these people talk about him, sharing their favorite memories of him, and she is mercilessly stalked by her own most insistent memories of John. They are boring and spectacular: trips to the grocery store, trips to far-flung places, wrestling playfully, stupidly in bed, fucking loudly and unashamedly in the hotel room with the view of the strip mall parking lot. Sharing a dinner of sausage and olives, washing dishes.

She can see his smile. She can hear his voice. *Claire. Come here. Hi beauty.* Singing to her: *Old black hen, is that you again, singing the bad luck lullabye?* Taunting her: *Claire-o Claire-o little bear-o, show me your lovely teeth.*

Will there be a time when she won't be able to remember his voice, his smile, his face? His hands.

She's here in this place—this place where he is not—and she is a widow. She has no husband. She has no job. She has no children. She's useless. She knows it. She lives in this tunnel of wind and sun and never ending vistas—*a fly between the screen and the glass.*

———

The butcher bird lives in this place. The tiny, elegant Loggerhead Shrike. She builds her nest by herself. Her sight is sharp and she is strong but her talons and beak and body are small. When she spots her prey—often larger than her—she captures it and impales it on a long thorny spike. The spike does the killing. The sun does the roasting and preserving. Time drains the poisonous prey of their venom, and she can return to their bodies for continual feasting, in her little spike-pantry. She is almost extinct, like most everything else.

THREE

She worked for the first few years of marriage—not very happily, but busily—until 30 arrived. And then she quit the last of her boring, unfulfilling jobs when she and John decided to try for a baby. She had never imagined not needing to work. For a while it felt as though she had won the lottery, and she hadn't even known that she purchased a ticket.

She was blissful in anticipation of motherhood, sure she would put every part of herself—even and especially her intellect—into thoughtful parenting. She was elated to leave the strictures of the work-world behind, secretly proud of John that they didn't need her income to survive, eager to spend her days doing the things we tell ourselves we'll do when time—more time—someday turns up.

But the baby itself never materialized, and with each passing year Claire was further from her working self and more fully realizing herself as something approaching a housewife, always almost about to have a baby. Or so she hoped. Hoped desperately, sometimes.

She didn't know what parenthood would bring, but she knew she wanted to kiss pillowy cheeks, to tuck little bodies into bed, to listen through the door for the contented and even breathing of total exhaustion. She wanted to know how to live for someone other than herself, to understand her limits and her breaking points. She wanted to be freed from the tyranny of always thinking about herself, her comfort, her desires, her needs, *herself.* And she was bored; her life needed stakes.

Her working life had offered none of the meaning and fulfillment she'd hoped it would. School couldn't do it, work couldn't do it, money couldn't do it, marriage couldn't do it. Maybe a baby would?

One mostly inconclusive session at a fertility clinic was all John had needed to say he wouldn't go down the IUI, the IVF, the force-it-into-being road. Male sperm counts are at an all-time historic low, and that's a fact; they just needed to wait and keep trying, he said. Claire couldn't disagree more. Why not do every possible test, have everything looked at, while we're still young? she'd argued, unconvincingly. *In five years we might not be able to afford it. In five years we might be gone.* Why not give it everything now?

They didn't fight about it, but for weeks, as Claire tearfully peed on ovulation detection strips each morning, she imagined convincing John, fighting and winning him over with her sorrow and her hot, lurching tears. But they were in the grey realms. Nothing was wrong with either of them, as far as they could tell. And he did not know the depth of her longing for a child. How could he? He was a powerful man with a beautiful wife and home and an important job and friends. A gulf opened between them.

Could they feel it? Did they know it? Had she been too proud to tell him? Would it have mattered to him?

What could she do? Drag him to the clinic after threatening divorce? Somehow implant the same desperate desire for parenthood in him? No, that wouldn't do. Even in her desperation she knew that each had to want a baby as much as the other, and that she wouldn't raise a baby as *hers* while her husband read the news and drank his scotch and absentmindedly patted the head of the child when it toddled over to him.

Most days she was pretty sure they had a good thing going, the two of them, baby or no baby. Why bother upsetting it? Why bother upsetting him? And so they tried and waited, tried and waited. *Dutiful* is how she felt, without being able to admit it to herself. She didn't yet know that duty breeds desperation.

Dutiful like Penélopê. Dutiful and desperate like all of them. All those depictions—those significations—that she knew so well. Anna Karenina threw herself on the train tracks. Ophelia drowned herself. Juliet drank the poison. Jocasta, Antigone, Emma Bovary, Hedda Gabler, Bertha Mason (how many more are there?), *they all knew it.*

Knew what? she wonders.

She remembers watching him when he didn't know she was looking, trying to read his mind. She remembers watching her belly, wishing she could somehow listen to it, willing herself to hear the movement of cells that she hoped were dividing deep within her. Probably, she realizes now, John had never really wanted a baby. He won that argument, or time won it for him. Or they had never even had the argument to begin with; John ran the clock out, knowing his position was the default position and that the little fights were just for show.

FOUR

The service is over. Some people are already leaving, others are talking in small groups or lining up to see John's parents and Claire. No one knows the protocol.

Andrew has a hand on Luke's left shoulder in a small gesture of affection. Claire looks at the hand, the shoulder, their faces. Andrew and Luke are looking at each other and Andrew is standing tall, his face warm and open, his gaze transmitting something to Luke that she can't make sense of.

Luke's eyes are clear and bright, but he does not seem entirely present. He looks as though he's just been knocked down—dazed and trying hard to focus. Claire can count on one hand the number of times Luke and John spent time together, just the two of them, but Luke looks as though he is dumbstruck by the loss of John.

There are other friends here, but she needs to focus on these two. She doesn't have the strength for the rest. She knows these two won't expect her to be anything other than herself. If being only oneself is even possible.

Claire loves these boys, these men, whichever they are. They love her, probably. Claire and John and this other two were never a closed circle, an overly tightly-knit group, but their years of shared history appear now to Claire as the history of family. They stand before her, waiting to put their arms around her, to be near her, to offer and examine their anguish.

It was always Claire and the boys. She has her female friends and likes and loves them; she's never been a woman who avoids friendships with other women. She's been cautious around the women who say they don't like women.

She's rarely been competitive with other women, but then, she rarely finds herself with them. Who have I been spending time with, she wonders. Herself.

———

They've all mostly kept in touch. Greeted each other with hugs at gatherings, shared late-night bingeing and soul-baring, inquired about the status of family members or exes, made efforts to see each other when in the same location. Her house—and John's—was the place for them to gather in recent years, whenever they could. No one they knew had substantial money, the kind to guarantee safety, but she and John had recently been the ones with the little bit of money, so they were the ones to cook the big meals, to play host and hostess, to buy the occasional plane ticket for the friend who wanted desperately to see them or to find the courage to leave a failing relationship, to take shelter in homes that weren't their own. They were not parents to their friends, no matter how paternalistic their love and care for them. For John especially, this was the necessary arrangement. He did not like relationships with uncertain borders.

Why had it always been this way? she wonders. Had he taken pride in flaunting their relative success—the fact that they could sometimes buy fresh produce, sometimes run the air conditioning year-round? Had he unintentionally, unwittingly pushed their friends away with his brazen offers of help, his insistence that he host and plan and take the reins? Maybe. She can't say.

Who are these men? she wonders when she looks at them. Luke the taut, straight-backed conveyor of honesty, Andrew the lurching seduction machine.

John had always resented Andrew. Who wouldn't? Andrew who shows up where and when he wants, often unannounced, usually with a new girlfriend or boyfriend who never seems to have been made privy to his plans. And John's careful plans, his routines, his schedules could never stand in the face of Andrew's energy. John wanted to know how many seats to reserve at the restaurant, how many bottles of wine to buy, what time he could expect to get to bed, if there would be a large enough party to justify the cost of the chicken he wanted to roast, if he'd be able to squeeze in a little more work before meeting up or going out.

Andrew has never been particularly attractive, but he has something else—the kind of something that can be sensed but not often made sense of. Andrew stalks the world. People find themselves drawn to him without understanding why. His intensity is a vortex and it functions like an undertow. Claire and everyone else knows this all too well. He is skilled at devastation. He knows this.

Andrew would bail at the eleventh hour, leaving an empty seat at the dinner party, an unoccupied hotel room, or he would arrive with two dates, each confused by the presence of the other. John would be sad and angry, not understanding why his friend couldn't demonstrate his affection in the ways he understood. Why couldn't Andrew just be legible? John would say he'd had it, that this was the last time they made plans with Andrew, but then Andrew would show up two days later, showering John and everyone else with his love, taking over the cooking, cleaning the house, inviting John's parents over for a last-minute drink and charming them, reading his poetry, dancing and singing, happy to make a fool of himself for the entertainment of everyone else.

Andrew dragged them outside one night, despite the heat, despite the approaching dust storm a few hundred miles away, and he identified all the stars in the sky. It had been years since Claire had studied the night sky. They sat in the gravel and Andrew made up a story for them, as though they were his children, about John and Claire and Andrew and a few others living in a colony on Mars, a blissfully misshapen family living at the edge of everything, keeping each other alive on love and beautiful bioengineered tomatoes and a library of poetry that he would hand-select for every one of them.

They never knew which Andrew to expect. Too often Andrew would arrive late, get drunk too quickly and ignore his dates, begin watching Claire or someone else who was not his date—man or woman, it didn't much matter to him—just a little too closely, making everyone uncomfortable. He would drink more, ignoring the resentment and frustration that made the room increasingly prickly and quiet.

His drunkenness would tip from sloppy into dangerous, and John would help him or force him over to the couch or the bed while Claire distracted their friends and Andrew's date or dates. She would pour them more wine, serve them dessert, turn up the music, suggest they all go out for the rest of the night. She would try her best to charm them like Andrew did, but she could never do it. Claire was so often jealous of him, of his mind, the self-possession that made concern for others unnecessary. She had always wondered whether it was self-absorption or a kind of selflessness—maybe a form of it she couldn't quite make sense of—that made him this way.

She remembers a night last year when she got up from the table to the clear the dishes and Andrew joined her in the kitchen, grabbing her wrist and hissing in her ear that he would give anything, anything she wanted, to watch her undress. She was taken aback; he was careful not to cross this particular line with her, knowing their friendship likely couldn't survive it. She hadn't known what to say. She looked at his face, removed her wrist from his grip, and silently left the kitchen. He stared long and hard at her back, watching her sneak away. He returned to his date at the table and kissed her cheek.

Later that night, in bed, Claire wondered: *Had he meant it?* Had he been drunk and high, had he been messing with her?

Andrew lives near them—near *her*, now. He has a bungalow a few towns over. The smallest yard, a flagstone patio, the house some version of an adobe with ancient, boxy air conditioning units in the windows, all of it run-down and un-cared-for.

When John and Claire moved here from the city a few years ago, the three of them were woozy with excitement to spend evenings together remembering that they were still sort of young. A few times they got stoned and fell asleep in the living room together. It was nice to let Andrew lead the way.

She had always been surprised that Luke and John weren't closer. Like John, Luke had always been responsible. Dependable.

At 25, Luke fell in love with an older woman and plunged headlong into a life of serious adulthood. Within the span of six or seven years, he had gotten married, had two kids, divorced. It was born, it grew, it grew some more, and then it died.

Claire remembers watching him through all of it, marveling at how well he seemed to be handling himself.

There were only a few fleeting moments in the year after the divorce when it seemed he was weighed all the way down by failing at a life he didn't know if he wanted or not. It was then that he wrote her a letter that offered an ultimatum. It troubled her, but she sensed that she might be foolish to take the letter too seriously. He was underwater, after all.

Luke surfaced. Claire knows he will probably always surface. *Men like him have every reason to surface.*

He has partial custody of his kids, he lives near them and his ex-wife, and they are at least friendly with each other. It was almost an amicable divorce. He has a good job for someone without an advanced degree, and he has friends who care about him and two brothers he has always loved and confided in. Luke understands, unlike the rest of them, that whatever fulfillment a job may or may not offer, being able to feed the kids will do more in the way of satisfaction and contentment than a job on its own ever could.

He has a lean face and quick eyes. Claire has always thought of his eyes as watchful. *They tell you how engaged he is—they tell you that he's listening.* His eyes give him away as a listener.

He knows things she does not yet know. She could usually sense it when she saw him—he saw things she could not. But she didn't yet understand why he knew what he knew. She didn't understand that as his life and his heart had been split apart, he had looked at the fragments and figured out which mattered most to him— which were worth the effort of keeping. He and Claire had been so close in their youth.

The divorce was nearly finalized when he spent a night drinking and thinking of her, putting pen to paper, mailing a letter to her as though the mail were reliable—as though there were still options outside of electronic communication. He told himself that they were good friends, trying to convince himself that it was just a friendly letter. But it was pointless. He knew the letter was a dangerous one. It called upon the ghosts of their pasts, the two of them seated on couches at endless parties, talking and smiling and trading their favorite Leonard Cohen lines, singing together, giggling like teenagers. He took a gamble and invoked one of those favorite lines:

> *I hear that you're building your little house,*
> *deep in the desert.*
> *You're living for nothing now.*
> *I hope you're keeping some kind of record.*

He knew that if John saw it, their friendship would be over.

He had been made so vulnerable by failing at what felt like every aspect of his life. Did he have anything left to lose?

She never wrote back. On that account, again, he should have known better. What was she supposed to say? *I'm here! Come and get me. Save me. Save me from myself. Your enemy is sleeping and his woman is free.* No. No such letter was sent.

Nothing was sent.

She was desperate to reply, but she didn't know how. He

wouldn't have sent it if there was no reason to send it. He knew it wouldn't fall on deaf ears. Maybe he knew she couldn't respond, but he also knew that she was not unreceptive. He kept waiting for a belated response—a brief text, a friendly email—but nothing came. He tried not to lose sleep over it. She kept waiting for the right response to come to her, but nothing came. She would stare at his handwriting—*it is strange to see handwriting now*—and she would wonder what he had been hoping for.

She spent days sitting on the front stoop of her little house, wondering as the sun boiled her insides: *Had he meant it?* Had he been lonely and devastated, had he been using the memory of her to prop himself back up?

And then John died. Someone living stopped living. It happens everyday.

She called Andrew right away. He lived close—she knew he could find a way to get to her quickly. They spent the afternoon sitting together in silence. Neither of them could find a way to speak. Andrew would have suggested going outside if it weren't for the heat. Silence is easier to maintain outside.

Claire's phone buzzed and rang nonstop, and she just watched as it vibrated across the surface of the table, moving of its own accord. Eventually she asked Andrew for a ride to John's parents' house, knowing she shouldn't drive herself.

The silence continued during the drive. She was

thankful for it. Andrew watched her closely, wondering if she was thinking anything at all.

Andrew reported John's death to Luke, calling him from the driveway of John's parents' house as he watched Claire climb the stairs to the front door and knock on it, as though she were just stopping by on any day, any day like any other.

Luke called Claire and she didn't answer. He texted her and he emailed her. He hoped she wasn't alone. His impulse was to drive to her immediately, to scoop her up in an endless hug, to take her somewhere, anywhere, but he knew he had no right to do so.

He got drunk at a bar and cried there on his stool—his first time crying in public. He loved John. He loved John despite and because of his possession of Claire. John was the kindest piece of shit he'd ever known.

Yes, he loved John, but in his more suspicious moments he wondered if John hadn't stuck himself and Claire in the desert on purpose—keeping both of them busy—he with work and building a full life, and Claire with living for nothing but him, so that she could never leave him. So that he would have control of her, hiding her in plain sight.

Luke found himself thinking of all the times John had been dismissive of the rest of the world, of the pain and the terror that everyone other than people like him— people with his luck—felt, and the stakes of such dismissiveness seemed suddenly dangerously high to Luke. He felt fear for Claire. Had John been cruel to her? Had he found the letter and been additionally cruel?

But John was dead now. How much of it mattered?

Does any of it matter, with fresh disaster looming every day?

FIVE

Disaster. The long, slow disaster of life now, life here, life then, life there.

The news of the disaster unfolded so slowly, so methodically, over the course of Claire's entire life, that she and everyone else never knew it was coming. It was never coming, in fact—it was always already there, just growing.

It is hard for organic bodies—no matter how large—to see their own growth.

She has food and shelter. Most of her friends and former colleagues still have food and shelter.

Will a sinkhole open up and swallow them? Will those starving in the Southern Hemisphere come for them and their food? Will the vast fields of greenhouses collapse under the weight of a massive multi-day hailstorm? Will those in power decide it's no longer worth the effort to keep the rest alive?

We can't look at it head-on, Claire and everyone else knows. Husbands die and wives grieve and it's the same as it's always been. Looking at it head-on makes the bottom fall out. She spends a lot of time and energy trying not to look at it head-on. There is so much she can't look at, so much she doesn't see.

You can ignore everything your body tries to tell you. You can just stay inside—no one will hold it against you.

The canned food isn't too bad. The air quality isn't unbearable. The summer heat is painful, but it's sort of always been that way anyway. There have always been throw-away people, there have always been empires. It's beyond fixing—all of it. Why bother with anything but a shrug in response?

Same as it's always been.

SIX

Claire has her own favorite memory of Luke. It is hers and hers alone. She's certain Luke doesn't remember it. John knew nothing of it. She returns to it again and again, like a song she knows by heart, not letting herself care that it's an old memory. *Why do I bother with it?*

Why does she polish it and keep it in her pocket like a little jewel? Because it feeds her narcissism, her self-obsession? John loved to tease her for her narcissism, as though she were the only narcissist, as though it were some unique feature of her personality.

The memory. *THE memory. Is it anything more than a reminder that there's nothing that cannot be lost?*

They were at university, kids playing at being adults—kids who had not yet needed to confront the disaster. Luke had been given a large quantity of Vicodin. A girl in one of his classes who harbored a crush on him had broken her leg. She had shown up in class, leg proudly encased in plaster, half of her pants shortened extremely to accommodate the cast. She bared that creamy, visible thigh in plain view of Luke, and tossed a small bag his way. When he caught it and took a minute to assess its contents, he sheepishly thanked her and said how he hoped her leg would heal quickly. It was a weeknight and there was another party—as there always was—and as good a time as any to put the pills to use.

Scarcity seemed an impossibility then, even and especially scarcities of joy.

As Claire remembers this night, Luke got too close to the brink with the help of some small white pills. As Luke understood the night while it was unfolding, he got more than just Claire's attention. He got her affection. But he got it in a cowardly way, he knew at the time. He made himself helpless in her presence, knowing she would step in to help, and then he made himself more helpless, manipulating her as best he could. Not that his attempt was a smashing success. But it was some kind of triumph, he knew. A small triumph. There's no big triumph for those who can't be in full possession of themselves.

For Luke, this was the beginning of a long night of feeling dejected, feeling un-fixably, eternally alone, hopeless. It was her fault. There she went, pressing herself neatly into a circle of glowing faces, talking excitedly about the week's successes, her small-ish body in her small dress, her long hair held back in a series of small, interlocking tangles. Luke couldn't help but feel that Claire had never known loneliness, at least not like he had. Alone at the table. *Alone in the middle of a party.* Alone the way he might always be, he knew.

As the night wore on, Luke kept his distance from Claire,

watching her only occasionally as she drank, laughed, sang at the top of her lungs, hugged her friend Gina, looked in Gina's eyes with love and care. Meanwhile, Luke tucked in to his pills. They slid down his throat with ease.

After his first Vicodin and vodka tonic, he had few cares. After his fourth or fifth V&VT, as he was now calling them, every care, every concern he'd ever had was gone. Disappeared. Like Los Desaparecidos, whom he'd learned about in his South American politics class just this week. With the help of his V&VTs, he had silently, stealthily murdered his concerns, his worries, his small, nagging anxieties.

At some point, Claire realized that Luke had been sitting in the same chair at the kitchen table for over an hour. He looked so thoroughly immobile, so perfectly still, that Claire wondered if he had in fact been sitting there all night. Luke's head moved slowly to the table, as if detached from the rest of him, and rested on the table-top. He made a move to sift through his pockets, but his hands and fingers were so clumsy and slow that he could only manage to brush the exterior of his pants, some-where in the region of his pockets. His head still on the table, Luke began to drool. His eyelids fluttered and closed, fluttered and closed.

Sensing trouble, she said, "Someone help me get him to the bathroom."

Those in the kitchen hoisted Luke from his chair and half-dragged half-carried him to the nearest bathroom. They stuffed him in the bathtub and turned on the shower, each of them trying, despite their varying levels of intoxication, to simultaneously sober Luke up and determine what the problem was.

"What'd he do? Did he drink that whole bottle of vodka?"

"Those pills! He had those pills!"

"Luke! How many did you take?"

He was not unresponsive, but all he could manage was a mumble. The water from the showerhead continued soaking him, pushing his hair into his face.

Glancing between his body and the doorway, watching his eyes shut tight, Claire said, "Give us a minute."

The rest filed dutifully out of the bathroom, glancing behind them as they went. On her way out, Gina said, "I'll be right outside, Claire. Shout if you need me. Just shout."

Claire kneeled next to the tub, turned off the water, and began stroking Luke's head, moving his hair out of his eyes. "Shit. Luke. What did you do to yourself?"

He managed another mumble and began attempting to shift onto his side. His coordination was so lacking, and the tub was so slick that he kept slipping onto his back as soon as he got any purchase. But it was clear he needed to turn onto his side or lean his head over the tub. She saw urgency and fear in his eyes. Claire reached into the tub and maneuvered Luke onto his side as best she could. He began vomiting. His dinner and his many drinks and his undigested pills painted the side of the bathtub, splashing back onto him.

Once it seemed as though this first round of vomiting was over, she reached back into the tub, helped him onto his knees, and positioned him so that he could throw up into the toilet, or, barring that, outside the bathtub, on something other than himself.

"He's okay!" Claire shouted. "He's throwing it up now!"

"Good," was Gina's response. "Do you need my help in there?"

"Not now. I think there's more that needs to come out."

And there was. Luke emptied his body until dry heaves exhausted him. The bathroom had that horrible warm puke smell, and Claire had bits of his dinner on her hands. She stood up to turn on the sink, to wash her hands and arms. He had collapsed back into the tub, exhausted, wet and covered in his vomit.

"I love you, Claire."

Claire stopped rinsing the soap from her fingers, remaining silent.

He repeated himself, "I love you. You know I love you," eyes closed.

"Luke." Claire returned to the floor, leaning into the tub, again pushing the hair out of his face. "You won't say that in the morning. You need sleep."

"No I don't. I love you."

Claire sighed and called for Gina.

Together, Gina and Claire cleaned him up. They threw his clothes in the laundry room and borrowed some from one of the guys who lived in the house. They washed and dried him, combed his hair, made him drink glass after glass of water. They tucked him into an empty bed in one of the bedrooms, promising to check on him every hour. They were playing at taking care.

After Gina had left the room, Claire lingered for a moment, waiting to see if Luke would say it again, hoping he would, knowing he would. He did.

Quietly, he said, "I love you Claire."

Claire knew it was true. She wanted his love. She had no intention of returning it. The audacity we have—she can see it now—when we're young and we throw away love, not understanding that it mostly doesn't come back and that it's rarely abundant.

She climbed into bed with him. He was sinking rapidly into recovery sleep, but she stayed there with him, his warmth radiating under the blanket, his breathing finally smooth and even. She touched his head.

She would take his love and run with it. She would let it make her wanted, noticed.

Later that year, when she would meet John and feel intimidated by his strength and intelligence and power, she would remember that Luke wanted her, maybe even loved her. She would use his admission to find the confidence to pursue John, to make him hers.

—————

Today she can see a corner of this memory and pull its warmth toward her. Not quite self-obsession then. Self-defense. Survival.

She can see that their friendship is not as one-sided as the favorite memory would suggest. She sees him now and knows that she loves him too, differently, newly, these many years after that intoxicated admission. She needs the memory because she needs the opposite of death.

Luke and Andrew are still standing there, looking at each other. They are alive. She is alive too. What would happen if she told them to climb into bed with her? What would happen if she grabbed their hands and led them into the parish house behind the church, this church she's never before entered and never cares to see again?

SEVEN

The shit is coming for all of us; life will gladly break us, *better take your diamond ring and you better pawn it babe.* Isn't it nice to pretend though, just for a while, that it won't happen? she thinks. *What else is youth for?*

This is what youth is also for, she thinks, at the funeral, as she is swarmed, offered love: being wasted. Youth is all waste. Pure waste. Wasted energy, wasted beauty, wasted love, wasted everything.

Her youth was wasted on a man who's now dead. Her love was wasted on the absence of a child. Her beauty was wasted on all the love or lust she couldn't or wouldn't accept. Soon she would tip past desirable into pathetic. It only takes a few years from here to reach pathetic. Her expiration date is approaching. Every woman has one, doesn't she?

These are dangerous thoughts, she knows. And soon

whatever's left of everything we can make use of on this planet, in this place, will be wasted too. We can't seem to stop the wasting. With this an additional frame arrives, fleetingly—the situation of her sadness, the geopolitical, historical location of some of her despair. *How pathetic to think it matters.*

Maybe Luke had been right, maybe that letter was the truth, maybe she had been living for nothing, for the past few years and every year of her life.

But no, that can't be right, she tells herself. She won't let the bottom fall out. She'd been living for John—for love —and he'd been living for her, and together they'd been living for their shared dreams and goals and friendships and the joy of simply living. *This must be right.*

———

But the terrible fact remains that her husband's death is the first event—the first *experience*—to involve her and not her husband (strangely, despite that it's *his* death), to seduce her out of the humdrum, in many years. Too many years. It's the way it goes—the way it's gone. She can feel the nihilism creeping slowly in.

———

Here are these men, her two friends. *Why have they remained so staunchly single?* Even when they were entangled in momentary or long-term relationships, they were still single men. It was never because of her that they remained unchained. She knows this.

And yet. They are watching her, hugging her, taking her

hand in ways she suspects they never could have, or would have, were John still alive. They are too attentive for this to be mostly about grieving the dead friend, comforting the grieving wife.

They have waited long enough. Now that he is gone, they can begin admitting what they have wanted for many years. Slowly.

Slowly. The admission begins with the eyes, moves to the hands. Each finds a chance to touch her shoulder or give a hug. She can feel their desire moving through her in waves, like music. *This is exhausting,* she thinks.

Pressing themselves against her, each unknowingly admits what he wants. *Do they know how easily they give themselves away? Is she imagining this? Is she mad with grief? Why does it seem as though they're here to claim some prize they think they've won? Surely she is mad with grief.*

If they are here, done waiting, why shouldn't she be done with the waiting too? She was married young. So young. At the height of her stupid girlish allure, limbs strong and graceful, hair long and unkempt. She was so young when she committed herself to John. Young enough to convince herself that she had simple desires.

She has unspent erotic capital. Plenty of it. An untouched savings account steadily accumulating interest. *Maybe I can find new ways to waste, new things to waste myself on.*

EIGHT

If she is mad with grief, Andrew will go mad with her. *Even if only for a night.* This she knows.

Andrew opens the door to his decaying station wagon. He glances quickly at Claire and jogs over to her side of the car, opening the passenger side door for her, as if realizing the mistake of not opening the door for a date. Claire is not his date.

The floor of the car is littered with newspapers, books, empty packs of cigarettes, a sweater or two, crushed and crinkly bottles of water, long ago drained of their insides. Only in the deepest interior corners of the seats is the fabric that vibrant, cheerful cerulean it once was. The car is a pale, muddy blue, dirtied by years of wear and tear, years of waiting in the sun, years of never being cleaned. It seems to have existed forever.

Somehow, Andrew makes a living. Claire has never been sure how he pays his bills or his rent, how he can afford gas money or food money or drug money—and there is always drug money. Andrew has been a poet for as long as she has known him. He seems incapable of being anything else. As far as Claire or anyone else can tell, Andrew did not grow into his life as a poet. He didn't find himself writing poetry one day, thinking *This is the job for me*. Nor did Andrew *make* this life of poetry for himself. It seems as though he had no choice in the matter. He simply wrote as he always did and trusted— without ever needing to say it to himself or anyone else —that he would never really have to do anything else.

Or he's just stubborn and lucky, Claire thinks. Maybe his stubbornness outweighs financial concerns, worries about the future, about security, about retirement. Does anyone have "retirement funds" anymore? But it's true that Andrew hardly makes any money from the poems he publishes. His two relatively well-received collections of poetry, *Rake in the Window* and *Small Sky*, both published in the same year, five years ago, bring him occasional royalties checks for barely more than $50.00.

He has no qualms about making up the rest of his living doing odd job after odd job, stitching his finances together like bricolage, ad hoc. This is the way it goes now for most. Andrew's neighbor grows weed and on occasion gives Andrew a little extra, gratis, so that Andrew can sell it to the local high school kids at a sizable mark-up. From time to time, Andrew bags groceries at the tiny Safeway in town. He'll do construction work. He's laid Saltillo tile in some of the wealthier folks' homes, ripped out their moldy, aging shower stalls, poured concrete for smooth, sloping driveways, re-shingled a roof or two with his contractor friends. He doesn't look like a poet—he looks like a roofer— someone who spends his days in the sun, working too hard, not eating enough, never bothering with sunscreen.

Andrew tells few people about this, but he also has a substantial savings account, sitting mostly untouched where his parents put it, or arranged to have it put, after their death. When their death did occur (first his father, then his mother, not more than two weeks later), nearly ten years ago, Andrew had become so used to his life and his hodgepodge finances that he decided to rely on the gift from his parents only when he needed to, when he wouldn't be able to make rent or was threatened with a shut-off notice from the gas company.

Claire has occasionally let herself wonder if the gift from Andrew's parents—a gift he always knew would come one day, though he couldn't have imagined how early in his life it came—is the reason he spent his days writing poetry to begin with. Successful or not, he had little to lose. *Just how bourgeois is he?*

Andrew drives Claire to the small, quiet town where he lives. In the car, passing canyons and mesas and flat expanses of land populated only by Scrub Oaks and Junipers, she sees the massive sky ahead of her, behind her, above her, below her, surrounding her. The sky is the only thing that exists here. It's more living than the land. If only she can drink this sky in, she thinks. If only she can drink it and consume it and become pregnant with it. *This sky, this endlessness, this stupid, simple beauty.*

Stupidity is undervalued, she thinks. *Forgetfulness is undervalued. Ignorance is undervalued.*

Andrew stops in front of a bustling pizzeria, asking Claire if she's hungry. She is, or thinks she is, but can't quite be sure. She knows she should try to eat.

The entire town seems to be here tonight. The glow of the candles in their little red candleholders lights up the faces of all the eaters, talking and laughing in their cramped booths. Andrew and Claire wait for a table near the front door, sitting in stiff-backed metal and vinyl chairs, sipping from the small glasses of red wine the hostess has given them as an apology for the long wait. Andrew breaks the silence, asking Claire what she thought of John's service. The question doesn't quite catch her off guard, but she doesn't know what her response is. She says nothing, takes a small sip of wine. Again, Andrew is the one to speak first.

"The flowers and the prayers—all the little things—were nice. Maybe John wouldn't have cared about that, but he would have wanted his parents to be happy with those details."

"Yes, that's true." Even in death, John would still have wanted to please his parents, to see them happy. "But I think he would have enjoyed the stories the most. John always appreciated good talkers. Good story-tellers." *If he's gone, what does it matter what he would have enjoyed?* She can't find an answer.

"He was one of them, you know. A good talker. Story-teller."

"You think so?" she asks.

"Yes, absolutely. When he wanted to tell a good story, he told a good story. His audience was all ears. Remember that time he commanded an entire living room at that hippie house party in Flagstaff with his summer camp story? That was a fucking great story." He gives Claire a little smile.

"I remember. I guess you're right. I just don't think of John as a storyteller. A thinker, yeah, sorta." A long pause. "An appreciator of great stories, definitely. He used to tell me stories. Funny ones about his childhood." Another pause. "But he was quiet a lot, wasn't he? Most of the time I had no idea what he was really thinking, if he was *in* the conversation or if he was thinking about work or something else."

"Who isn't distant? I think he told you everything. *You* were everything to him."

"I know that." She doesn't want Andrew's reassurance— he is much better at giving other things.

Claire and Andrew are escorted to their table, empty wine glasses in hand. The waiter announces the evening's paltry specials, and they are both quiet for several uncomfortable moments before Andrew continues their conversation about John.

Tapping on the table's edge, he can't stop it from coming: "This hurts." A pause, with his large hand on his chest, and then, "We all loved him so much. It's hard to talk about him."

"This is hard for you? This is what your pain looks like?" Why does she doubt him?

"What *should* my pain look like?"

She was doing to him what she was afraid all the others —what *they*—would do to her. She wants Andrew's grief

45

to be readable. She wants a roadmap of pain. All pain. Now and forever.

"I'm sorry." She studies him because she's suddenly nervous.

"No, I am," he says. "I don't know what this is like. I don't know what any of this is like. Every death is different. My parents' death can't help me understand. Maybe we shouldn't talk about it just yet."

"Agreed. And I-" the words caught in her throat, "-don't want to talk about John right now. I have talked to myself about him endlessly, fucking endlessly, since he died. I can't keep doing it. I have to stop."

Andrew looks at her with concern. After a long pause, he says, "So are you tired of wearing black or what? Maybe break out the red? Some commemorative crimson? Yes, that's more mature and practical." *That's right* she thinks. *He doesn't linger. He never lingers.*

"Andrew." A smile broke out on her lips. "Jesus."

"Wanted to see you smile, that's all." He kicked her playfully under the table, giving her his goofiest grin in return.

With his kick and his grin, they are friends again. No longer just two grieving people, strangers to each other in their grief. Maybe they can grieve alone together.

"What are you working on right now?" Claire asks him. "Anything new?"

"No, not really" is his careful response. "Something that's kind of a short story, maybe eventually a novel. I don't know what it is right now. I've been writing a lot this past week, since-" about to violate their contract of twenty seconds ago, he stops himself, "I think I'm done with poems for a little while. I'm finding characters I want to spend more time with. People instead of ideas."

"That's great. That's really great. We always wondered if you'd ending up writing a novel."

"We?"

"All of us, I guess. Lots of your exes." She wants to see him squirm a little.

"Oh Christ, let's definitely not talk about any of them tonight, okay?"

"Yeah, fine. I don't care about them. You could write a good book, is what I'm meaning to say."

"Thanks, Claire." Another little kick under the table. Another smile.

She's not very sharp as the evening wears on and they eat across from each other. She's having trouble trusting what she thinks she sees in Andrew's eyes and face.

She picks at her pizza, she looks up to see him watching her. *What is that look?*

Desire so real it seems to have a physical presence. She's suddenly afraid. *How much wine have we had?*

As the waiter clears the last of their dishes and the restaurant empties out, Andrew rubs his hands together in a flourish of nervousness she hasn't seen him perform in years. It looks as though he has something to say that she doesn't want to hear. Frowning in the direction of his hands she says, "Why don't you just drive me home now? I'm tired. I should spend some time with John's parents tomorrow, before they go home."

"Yeah I'll drive you home." Another little hand-rub. "I have something in the car you might want. Maybe something to turn your brain off."

"Hmm?" Claire tries not to raise her eyebrows at him, tries not to let her fear show.

He continues, lowering his voice just enough to be discreet but not enough to be mistaken for being ashamed, "Pills. Just pills. They're painkillers essentially."

In the car outside Andrew's house, Claire feels strangely calm. *Why did I come here?*

"Well?" she asks him. *Maybe if we can pretend, for just a few moments, that we belong to each other—possess each other wholly—we can return to our lives intact.* Maybe she won't need to self-destruct. Maybe it can be this simple.

Andrew does indeed have pills—a small series of bags, each carefully labeled. He knows which go with which, how they'll interact, how she'll feel once they hit her. She doesn't like these small bags and their After School Special associations, but she knows she can trust Andrew's pharmaceutical knowledge, and she has already followed him into the house anyway, kicking her shoes off in the entrance, as though entering her own home.

The pills dance down her throat, and she doesn't have to

wait long for them to work; she's already had wine and not enough food. Sometimes it's the pain itself that finds a lover, and you're its small sad conduit.

They sit in his hot, desolate living room on his sinking futon, shades drawn low as the sun sets, until she blinks and finds she's capacious enough to accommodate the universe. She is fire, she is water. She wonders about a line in a song she used to know: *When you dance it is torture.*

She is plummeting but she doesn't have enough in her to fight it; she's tired of having control.

He takes her hand and they move silently to the bed. He presses his body into hers, takes her wrists in his hands as if to tie her to the bed with his long fingers. There's a rehearsed quality to his movements—he does this more often than her. She keeps blinking, wondering if everything will still exist when her eyes open.

Their clothes are on. She can't meet his eyes. He keeps pleading with her, "Look at me. Claire, look at me. Look in my eyes."

A small "No" is all she can manage.

Not because she is ashamed. Not because to meet his gaze would be to admit intimacy. Not because she needs to imagine a different face hovering above hers. She has always wondered what this would be like with him. She has never thought unpleasantly of what they might do alone in a darkened room. How does his intensity translate when his body meets another? It just happens that she is not in the room with him as it finally occurs.

She is swimming in the community pool, during the summer between her 7th and 8th grade years, with her sister, spitting water at her sister, marveling with her sister at how their hair really does look like a mermaid's when they're underwater. She is drinking a juicebox and lazing in the sun with her sister, braiding her sister's long, fine hair, getting pinched by her sister, with with with her sister. The pills are taking her to her little sister, her dear little sister, best friend, enemy, most and least trusted secret-sharer. No she cannot look in his eyes.

No, no I cannot. Why are they taking me here?

They would stay underwater for as long as they could, eyes open, gazes locked on each other. *One hard blink meant Go up now, two hard blinks meant Drink your tea and then go up.* They would surface and gasp for air. They would revel in the few moments when the heat was welcome, when it would warm their bodies chilled by the water. *Where is she right now? Does she know I'm seeing her? Can she feel it?*

I'm here, Dodo. I'm here. Are you here too?

This isn't going the way she wants it to—she doesn't want her sister right now. She wants to feel whatever Andrew wants her to feel, wants to be just a nameless thing to him, wants to live the dream of losing herself forever. But she can't.

"Oh baby baby baby. Beautiful fuckable" he is saying. He

has something he wants. He is present for it, lingering in it, running his hands along the length of her side and leg with focus. Clothes are off. *When did that happen?*

She has the clear sensation that she's moving fluidly between three or more levels of consciousness. She settles on one and closes her eyes. *Please let me have this.* This time, her little sister stays dutifully away, far away, and she fucks Andrew in a state approaching euphoria, with a dedication previously unknown to her. Andrew is crying. He is shouting her name and grabbing her body with his arms, rolling her from one side of the bed to the other, letting his tears stream onto their two bodies. Between choked sobs he says, "I could kill you. I need you. Oh Claire. My Claire."

He begs her to hit him. She obliges. She can't tell if he feels the sting of it. There's some script he seems to be following. She has no access to it but she will let herself do what he says. "Hit me again," he says. "Harder." Her hand prickles with heat and he says "Again, harder" and she cannot believe it when she feels the heat of her hand spread to the rest of her, slow and steady.

She hadn't thought before that when it's rigid like this, abandonment is possible because innovation is not. She has the clear thought that this is her first time really, actually having sex, actually fucking, and she watches as she notices that she is afraid and excited and more powerful, more destructive, than any other woman on the surface of the earth. The thought passes, slips away. She wants to kneel down and pray. To what she's not sure.

Andrew is hers. She is hers. Together they will fuck the world and themselves out of existence. Outside this room, the abandoned landscape is littered with abandoned buildings.

Can you slice me out of me? I don't want this body anymore.

In the morning, she sneaks a few fuzzy-headed, nauseated moments for observation. Andrew is deeply asleep, his naked torso stretched casually across his side of the bed. Claire looks at his skin. His dark brown skin and the few patches of hair splattered on his chest, haphazardly, without pattern. She looks at the hairs embedded in his ears, at the rich pink of his nipples. She touches him. He is warm, radiating warmth. *What if he were the dead one?* she thinks. *What if he were the dead one?* His body still here in this bed, but lifeless, limp, cold. Browned and naked and wicked and dead.

Andrew stirs, sensing eyes on him. He has the contentment of a confident sleeper. Like a cat, happy to be gazed upon while slumbering, stretching to offer up a limb for examination. He pulls Claire to him, draping her arm across his chest. He gives a little smile and falls asleep again.

For breakfast, he takes her to a diner he frequents. They sit next to each other, in that awkward teenage-intimacy way, on the plastic booth seat, and together they silently consume their hash browns and scrambled eggs. The waitress eyes her warily, nearly rolling her eyes at the fact of the two of them there, in that booth like adolescents. *He must bring all his women here.*

Sadness arrives quickly, and it lingers. She would like to cry, but she doesn't. Being wanted is not being loved. She knows this, knows this in the fiercely painful way we know things we can't admit, can't act on. Being wanted is welcome, she can admit this. Being loved can cancel out the need to be wanted. But if being loved is not an option, being wanted will at least keep the checking account active. Money has to keep flowing.

She wants to ask Andrew why she's here. She wants to ask the waitress. She wants to ask everyone: *What* am I doing? Here? As if Andrew—as if anyone—can answer for her.

Andrew offers his smile. *Still young in the face,* she thinks. The face of someone who's never made commitments. "You finally came to me."

"What?"

"Yeah, you did. You were ready." He shows no sign of remorse, no detectable shame in saying these words aloud. The closeness they had at dinner last night is gone.

Did she hate him or admire him for saying it?

She thinks for a moment. "I didn't come to you. You came to the funeral." Her voice has a sharpened edge. *There is no room in him.*

He shrugs at her—one small, casual gesture of dismissal. How can it be that even the man who has seen her most transgressive self is ready to reduce her to some pathetic caricature?

Why she didn't leave that small diner in a gasp of silent, righteous indignation she'll never quite know. Or if she knows, she will never be comfortable with what that knowledge reveals to her about herself.

Behind the conversation—from the spot where she observes herself—she remembers a class she took as an undergrad in college, and the professor who spoke eloquently and at length about the dangerous love affair we have with the Lost Little Girl trope.

"Think about every fairy tale! Every Disney film! Every song about the woman—excuse me—the girl, who needs saving! Think about how that girl is *made sexier* by the fact of her lostness. Think about it!"

But I am not a little girl, Claire thinks.

Anna Karenina threw herself on the train tracks. Ophelia drowned herself. Juliet drank the poison. Jocasta, Antigone, Emma Bovary, Hedda Gabler, Bertha Mason (how many more are there?), they all knew it.

Knew what?

NINE

It's late morning now. Almost midday. When Claire returns to her house—her house and John's—there are handwritten notes from John's mother and Luke. There are text messages and voicemails waiting on her cell phone, perched on the corner of the table where she uncharacteristically—absentmindedly—left it the morning of the funeral, yesterday morning. People are wondering where she is. How she is. Has she eaten? What does she need? Has the rain come yet?

She slinks inside, wilting from the heat, wondering if any of the neighbors have noticed her.

The note from Luke has been stuffed under the door, a half sheet of paper torn from a magazine. It says, simply: Call me. Me = Luke.

Her eyes scan the dining room and the kitchen, resting on the table in front of her. John built this table, with the help of his father, when he and Claire had finally moved into a house that had the space for a table, in a real dining room. Almost three years ago.

At this table they'd eaten countless breakfasts and dinners, lazy Saturday lunches. They'd hosted their friends for cocktails and snacks at this table. They'd eaten cold, unappetizing leftovers at this table. Next-day spaghetti, the noodles dried out and crunchy. They'd argued at this table. She had wondered if their child or children would do homework at this table. They'd opened their computers and tablets and planners and scheduled their weeks and months and years at this table. They'd made love on this table, once. It hurt. It's an ugly table.

A table. Their table. Claire now feels the horror of last night, as though she were feeling it for John. She knows it may be betrayal. *But, there is no John to betray. No John anymore,* she finds herself thinking.

She turns from the table and walks up the stairs to their bedroom, where their clothing and their chapstick and their slippers are housed. All the boring, unsexy possessions that made up their marital lives are still firmly in place. The novel John was halfway through sits on his nightstand, bookmark in place. His last glass of water too. *Should I leave them there forever?* she wonders.

John. Just the other day he was reading this book, drinking from this glass. How can it be that he won't finish the book, the glass of water? *How is it possible?* And then: *What is wrong with me? What is wrong with me? What is wrong with me?* She can't stop thinking these words. She thinks them so thoroughly that she startles herself when she hears her voice forming them. She is saying these words quietly, over and over, until her voice can no longer bear the strain of whispering, and she breaks into a shout. Shouting—*What is wrong with me?*—she sits down at the edge of the bed. The tears aren't coming. She doesn't know where they are.

She hears her phone ringing downstairs. Lacking the strength to answer it, but lacking the courage to continue ignoring people who want to see her, who need to know if she is okay, she moves swiftly down the stairs to the dining room. It's Luke. She lets out a small sigh.

"Hi, Luke."

"Claire?"

"Yes?"

With some happiness in his voice: "I thought I'd never reach you, old sport. Where are you?"

"I'm home. Just got here. Where are you? Sport? Old Sport?" She feels suddenly drugged, sleepy, like her limbs wouldn't cooperate if she tried to move them just now.

With a small laugh he says, "I'm staying at the Holiday Inn. They gave me a room with a mini kitchen and an ironing board—the deluxe divorcé suicide suite. You sound tired."

"Oh yeah?"

"Yeah."

Claire lets the silence on her end linger. Her word reserve is wiped out. "Maybe I am. Tired."

"I'm not going to be able to stay in town for long. I'm going to see John's parents later today. Are you free tonight?"

"I'm free tonight, yeah."

"Well, do you want-"

"No," she finds herself saying, "I'm actually not. Actually not free tonight."

"Okay. How about tomorrow? You wanna meet for breakfast? Take a walk after that?"

She realizes she can face Luke if only she can get some sleep, have a shower, eat some dinner. She agrees to meet him for breakfast tomorrow morning. She grips the phone in her hand, walks back up the stairs, pulls off her clothes—the same she wore to the funeral, the same she wore last night—and eases herself into the bed. She stares at the ceiling for a few minutes, forcing her eyes to stay open as long as she can, and then she is out.

―――――――――

When she wakes up the sun is rapidly descending. The air conditioner hums—it is always running, struggling to keep up with the demand. The phone is ringing again, its jaunty tune muffled under the covers. *My sister. Did I conjure this call?* She wants nothing more than to talk to her sister. But it will be no walk in the park.

Dacia and John were close for siblings-in-law. Claire knew her sister would never have missed John's funeral if she weren't overseas, if the 30 hours of traveling to get here to the Southwest at the last minute didn't cost more than 3 months' salary. And the funeral happened so quickly after John's death, she hardly would have made it in time.

The last time they spoke, her sister wept over the phone,

apologizing to herself and to Claire and to the now-dead John for not being able to make it to the funeral. So yes, Claire wanted badly to talk to her sister, but she knew she needed to brace herself for a Conversation. *It's strange that such complicated calculations can be made in the blink of an eye.*

"Hi Dodo."

"Hi Cee-cee. I miss you a lot."

"I miss you too Dodo. I wish you could be here." Claire's voice began to crack. *So here are the tears? Now? For my sister?* But it was so true it was making her stomach ache: she wanted her sister with her. She was so alone.

"I don't know what to say, about anything. I want to be there too." Claire could hear Dacia struggling to hold back tears. She was trying to keep her voice from quivering.

"I know you do. I don't mean to make you feel bad."

"I've just been worried about you. I can't sleep. I want to see you and see if you're okay."

"I don't know if I'm okay, Dodo. I don't know what I am."

"I know." Dacia took in a big breath. "Cee-cee, will you please take care of yourself? Because I don't think I-" She paused to let out a sob, and continued in the higher-pitched voice of someone fully crying, "Because I don't think I could live without you, Cee."

Dacia's tears brought on Claire's. "Dodo, I'm trying. I will. I will figure out how to take care of myself." *Am I lying?*

"Okay. I'm sorry. I'm sorry! I don't want you to be alone."

"It's okay Dodo." A very long pause, during which they both sigh. "It's okay."

When they finished the conversation and they choked out their goodbyes, Claire padded once again down the stairs, slowly, afraid of tripping and breaking her neck. She had to find something to eat. She found a can of sludgy lentil soup in the pantry, heated it up, took it upstairs to bed, and put on the television.

She remembered when most food was not canned, when the Co2 levels in the atmosphere and the consequent carbohydrate-density of plants hadn't yet required laborious indoor growing and canning operations. *We had a little balcony garden once.* Some peas and tomatoes they had tended with care. The soil was potted, she remembers, but it felt rich and silky.

Having the television in the bedroom had been a point of contention for Claire and John. Like any educated nearly-middle-class couple, or whatever they were, they both felt an unplaceable guilt for enjoying visual media. John had argued that they should be able to watch the evening news in their bedroom, if they wanted to. Claire made a show of worrying that a television in the bedroom was too intrusive, would interfere with sleep or whatever else they wanted to do in the bedroom. It should be a sacred place, she'd insisted. It *was* a sacred place, John also insisted, and having a television wouldn't change that. Claire relented, mostly because she too wanted to be able to watch the news in bed. Even news of the unfolding disaster was its own kind of comfort. The world did still exist out there, outside these walls. None of the old categories worked anymore, they were living on borrowed time like everything else, but if they paid careful enough attention to the facts of the disaster, they didn't need to *think* about it.

On an evening like this one, when all she wanted was distraction and soothing reminders that everything was exactly as it ought to be, she was never more thankful that John had pleaded his case. As she finished her soup and tucked herself further into the bed, the television sang her to sleep.

TEN

There was a time when John almost left her.

He told her later, when they were a more stable couple of many years, occasionally capable of having the difficult conversations, that it had happened back when they hadn't been together for long. They had gotten so serious so quickly, he explained, and he had awakened one morning—thinking maybe he had finally *come to*— and he was uneasy.

He was suddenly unsure if they should be so serious, if he should be doing this. What *were* they doing?

Was this a mistake? He watched Claire wake up and reach for a glass of water next to the bed. Was this the scene he would wake to every morning? Would this uneasiness linger? Would he wonder every morning from here on out if he had made an enormous mistake? Would this banality be his life?

Claire kissed John's head and got up. She asked him what he wanted for breakfast as she peed in the bathroom attached to their bedroom. He was flooded with dread. It swept over him and seized his stomach. His words caught in his throat when he tried to respond. As Claire lingered in the bathroom, he managed to say quickly, "Toast. Toast is fine."

He hurried out to the living room to check his email. This was his first year of life in the working world, as a recent graduate with no experience and everything to prove. He didn't like the thought of his life threatening his work, compromising the sanctity of his devotion to the career he was starting—hoping—to build. Devotion and duty were required.

He was distracted at work that day. He was short with his colleagues. He ate his lunch without realizing he was eating. He sat in a meeting feeling like a ghost—nothing to say, nothing to do, nothing that could matter to anyone. He envisioned his parents. Was that what he and Claire were starting?—a life like the one he had seen his parents have, together? Why did he feel such fear at the thought of it?

His parents had always had a mostly harmonious life together. They made a strong team, conferring and considering each others' opinions on the big decisions, fighting only occasionally, encouraging each other to pursue their interests and to spend time with their friends, and talking to each other, for the most part, like intelligent, thoughtful partners that each had chosen, and not like bored, dissatisfied, resentful co-workers stuck in co-habitation out of economic necessity, as the parents of so many of his friends seemed to. *Why*, then, was he afraid? What was this dread? He couldn't figure it out.

It ate at him all day, and by the time he returned home after work, he was no longer certain that he loved Claire, that he could possibly love Claire, or anyone else for that matter. He sat her down at the table before dinner, before they had even poured an after-work glass of wine, and told her he had something he needed to say.

"I don't know about this, Claire." He was met with a silence he couldn't immediately interpret.

"What about this?"

"I mean *us*. I don't know if I'm ready for this, for us."

Claire took this in for a moment, flipped her hair to the other side of her head, rolled her head down and then around as if to suggest the inadequacy of an eye-roll. "Jesus Christ, John. What the fuck. You think I'm certain? You think any of us are ever certain about anything? You wanna stay with me, stay with me. I love being with you. You know I love being with you. Don't pull this shit with me. Just go if you want to go." She paused and looked at him without flinching. *God she's young*, he thought. If there was more she needed to say, she wasn't going to say it tonight.

He saw a deep viciousness in her then that he'd never seen before. Not only could she take him or leave him, he thought, but if they stayed together, she would be able to slice him up with her eyes—just like this—for the rest of his life. Did he want this? How could he possibly want this?

She considered him again, letting her eyes linger on him, and then she stood up. She left the table, left the room. He couldn't have known how desperately she needed to be appearing to play it cool, to be fully in charge, to be far from breakdown.

Why hide this from him? Why not be honest? Why not share his vulnerability? Maybe it *was* her youth, her relative inexperience with serious relationships. Maybe it was her pride. Maybe it was that subterranean, always lingering fear of being alone, being exiled. A kind of death, to be sure.

As Claire left the room John knew immediately that he loved her. *Shit*, he thought, *I have to tell her I love her. She has to know or she'll leave.* He felt hollowed out—emptied —knowing he'd found someone to love, not knowing if he could stand to love her and live everyday with the grotesque and ordinary consequences.

Soon he'd be the guy who didn't mind finding a used tampon in the trashcan next to the toilet. Soon he'd be peeing in front of his girlfriend—or worse, shitting. Soon they'd be so bored with each other they'd get fat and not even be ashamed of it. If Claire were old and dying, would he wipe her ass for her? He didn't like the bodilyness of love, he was realizing. It was disgusting, all of it.

But now there was no mistaking it—he was in love. He didn't know how he could live without things he wasn't even sure he wanted. She had grabbed him.

Two nights later, when he made up with her in his mind, resigning himself to this thing they had—to following it because he couldn't not—he went to Claire in bed. He crawled in beside her, held her as she slept. He felt his breathing merge with hers, matching the pace of it as she stirred slightly.

He thought of the years of his life before Claire. School. Mostly school. So much schooling. Every capacity of his, every potentiality, every seed of aptitude had been measured to death, assessed until all interested parties were sure he would thrive and boldly face the pressures of late capitalism. Was he thriving? Was anyone?

Work was no different, he was discovering. It's just that the work world was less up-front about the measuring. Now there was little warning that it was coming; it was just never *not* coming. The quarterly performance reviews were one thing; the consistently evaluative tone of his supervisors, the need to promptly answer every hand-wringy email was another.

Could it be worth it? Could any of it possibly be worth it?

His worth was his utility, he was realizing. No one makes it out.

And utility was measured by the dollars he brought in, or might soon bring in, or might help others to bring in. All other aspects of him and his life mattered only insofar as they made that particular utility possible. It was stunning, really. How simple it was.

The exhaustion. It made him want to stay in this bed and sleep forever. Lie on some forest floor until the elements overtook him. Let a strong breeze nudge his body into the Grand Canyon. He would sail to the ground as his eyes caught one last blurry glimpse of the reds and oranges and browns of the striations, churning and swirling in his field of vision. Maybe he could kill himself. Why not? All the brilliant men did it, didn't they? Was he a brilliant man? He'd thought so—used to think so.

But all those luminaries, visionaries, beautiful artists—all the ones he looked to in order to learn how to live—the Kurt Cobains and Hunter S. Thompsons and Elliott Smiths and even, for a brief spell in college, the David Foster Wallaces—they threw themselves into the fire before they could see how hard it really got. Before they could see if what they assumed was too soul-crushing to face was in fact soul-crushing. Pussies.

Or maybe it was simpler than that. Maybe they didn't even opt out of any kind of responsibility; maybe they just gave up on life because they'd done all they needed to. They didn't throw themselves into any fires. They just stopped existing altogether, popped magically out of existence because they couldn't possibly exist slavishly. They were only here to work their magic, and then they were taken away. He didn't really believe this, did he? It sounded awfully supernatural. Religious almost.

But there was a seed in him that most of this world couldn't detect. Claire saw it, knew it. Some friends knew it. A sliver of his core that existed for him and his pleasure and the pleasures he may offer others. It was gloriously, perfectly lazy, unresponsive, unconcerned with the outcomes of all the *measurements*, oblivious to how exceptional he was in the eyes of most who knew him. It knew that everything would end soon and that they might starve tomorrow like everyone else, but it sought joy nonetheless. It raised a middle finger to the work he had to do, it helped him sleep soundly, it allowed his occasional self-indulgence, and when its little flames were fanned it wanted nothing more than to lie in the sun on a beautiful afternoon. With Claire beside him. He saw it now. *We are all lost at sea,* he now knew, *but I want to be lost with Claire. Without her, I'd be alone in my boat. Nowhere, alone.*

He understood why he was in love, what separated being in love from enjoying a few good fucks and laughs and moving on. He wanted to be useless with her. She had somehow worked her way into this usually-invisible sliver of him, as a baby's DNA floods the mother's bloodstream and migrates to the organs to plant tiny outposts of an unknown purpose, where they will stay forever.

To find any love is to be forever in the debt of beauty, she knows now. It cannot help but transform. It requires bleeding. It always aches. Love is not far from fear.

That she knew all of this, that they had just a few years ago had the kind of conversation that compelled John to reveal all this to her was crucial. She couldn't forget it— any of it. *John was complicated and beautiful, and he loved me.* She can't let herself forget it. She wants desperately to find some way to forever remember it. *He loved me despite the fear.* Even as she sleeps tonight, she is working frantically to find novel methods of preservation. *All any of us has is each other.*

Don't leave.

ELEVEN

Claire the widow wakes the next morning with plenty of time to shower and dress before meeting Luke for breakfast. She wears her most unflattering pants—the pants John called fat-lady pants, because of their elastic waist and their ample material in the buttocks and hips —and a plain t-shirt.

Penélopê undid her weaving work each night, hoping to buy herself some time, didn't she?

She finds new ways to deal with the heat, along with everyone else, as it increases each year. She pulls her wet hair back into a knot. She applies a small dab of lipstick and smudges it on her lips. She is still conscious of not looking done, made-up.

Today a widow might not wear black for months or years, but she can demonstrate her grief with a lack of self-care. Everyone knows this. Best not to violate too many widow taboos. Best, also, not to slide into that total absence of self-care: widows with unwashed hair, widows with smelly armpits, widows in the same clothes for days, widows unable to speak.

Dropping her phone into her purse, slipping her shoes on, grabbing her keys, Claire leaves the house. She will be on time for her breakfast with Luke. There's another thing to be aware of: the widow with no sense of time. The widow always late or early, wandering into places as though she's perpetually lost and confused, floating around like some dull, nearly-middle-aged ghost.

Luke is seated next to the window at a small two-person table when Claire arrives. He is studying a menu, gripping a mug of coffee as it rests on the table. He looks tired. Sad. Maybe anxious. He sees Claire approaching and does his best—it's a valiant effort, really, and it isn't lost on Claire that he is trying this hard for her benefit—to smile at Claire as though he's happy and she looks great, as though they are just two friends meeting for breakfast. As though he's not divorced and she's not widowed. Just two happy, healthy thirty-somethings with only movies, music, and mutual friends to chit-chat about.

Luke stands and gives Claire a long hug. Claire stiffens in his arms, unsure of what's coming.

After the eggs and the toast and the bacon arrive, and after the coffee is quickly drunk, Luke stands, leaving most of the food on his plate untouched. They've hardly exchanged a word.

She can't stop thinking of the letter. The letter. She thought she had put it out of her mind. *But here he is.*

He drops two quarters into the jukebox and looks back at Claire before pressing the buttons to select the song.

He walks toward Claire, hand outstretched, asking her for a dance. She takes his hand, as she has surely taken his hand many times before, innocently, in the presence of everyone else and her husband.

Otis Redding is singing to her. *To* her. Just her. His arms are longing for her, longing to hold her. She will let him hold her. She drapes her arms across Luke's neck, letting him pull her closer, letting her head rest on his shoulder. The stiffness has drained from her. They dance like eighteen-year-olds at prom. They dance like they will never be held again.

"You piece of shit," she says quietly. He knows this weak spot of hers: Otis Redding on a jukebox, dancing in plain view of everyone, where no one else is dancing, arms around her, holding her tighter and tighter. *How many weak spots do I have? Does he know them all?*

His mouth moves to her neck. She begins to shake in his arms.

"No, not the neck," she whispers as her eyes close.

They keep dancing, slowly—cautiously—but he removes his right arm from around her body and moves it abruptly to the small space between their bodies, his open palm on her chest, just below her neck. He moves it up to her throat, applying a slight pressure, and then slides it around to the back of her neck, applying even more pressure. He is grabbing her neck. He grabs her neck.

She turns her mouth to his face and licks his cheek, lost to desire. She can feel the roughness of his stubble on her tongue.

His cologne smells like her father-in-law's.

She returns to herself and sees what she's doing, what Luke is doing. She pushes herself out of his arms and returns to the table.

Luke follows and they both sit down as though nothing out of the ordinary has happened, as if they've both just returned from the bathroom. She has to be direct, she realizes. *I can't let this slide from my control.* She can hear the letter in her head as though he were reading it to her, as she has read it to herself a hundred or more times.

You are beautiful, with flames always shooting from your mouth, knives from your eyes. You are beautiful in your imperiousness, your vulnerability made into arrogance. You are beautiful when you're transfixed, bewitched—seducing all, unbeknownst to you—even with your hand covering your mouth, eyes behind sunglasses. I can always see you.

"What did you want to talk about?" she asks, businesslike.

"Talk about?" he responds, with pain in his voice, as though he had walked into a formal interview when he had expected a friendly conversation. "I wanted to see you before I go. I wanted to see if you're okay. I...wanted you to know I'm here for you. I want to help."

You are beautiful when you speak. I like you best sober— laughter almost always pushing through your careful speech. Did you know you're always careful with me? Even your words are measured out and set down just so. You are emotionally closed to me—a sealed room—but I want another life in which I can be a person you let in.

"I don't know how you can help. I don't—" her voice trails off.

She feels her eyes filling with tears. Luke's strange warmth is undeniable. It stings. She wipes the tears away quickly. "I just don't know what I need. I don't know how anyone can help."

> *I can't even meet your gaze sometimes. When we were just kids and we spent all those nights hovering at the edges of the party, huddled on the couch together, I would have to lean hard into drunkenness to look you in the face. Did you know this? Have you always known this? It has always felt like an honor to be looked at by you, to be considered by you. I have always felt special—un-ignorable—when your eyes were fixed on me.*

"John would want me to do what I can. So I'm here. I love you both."

The mention of John's name brings the tears back to the surface. Of course she can cry in front of Luke. If she does it enough he'll probably join her. *That fucking warmth of his.* He reaches for her hand across the table, and once again she accepts, placing her palm on his. She closes her eyes for a moment. She can't not. *The heart wants to explode far away, where nobody knows.*

"I feel tired," she whispers. *How much can I want at one time? How much can I contain?* Is she bursting? Women are not supposed to want like this—no one is supposed to want like this. It's causing her to circle back around to the grief and feel it twice, once as grief, twice as grief plus guilt.

I have always wanted your eyes to flash at me, telling me that we share some unspeakable secret. There've been times when I think I've wanted nothing more than a life of being looked at by you. Are you shaking your head at this? I am at least smart enough—just barely smart enough—to know that I shouldn't say these things to you. And yet. What can I say? We have known each other for so long. I've waited for these things to leave me—for you to leave me. It hasn't happened. Maybe I'm confusing my love for you as a friend with something else, some other kind of love. I'm not sure. I don't know. I don't know if I'm kind or cruel. Should I be silent?

Luke looks at her with wide-open eyes, intensity in his face. He has advice to deliver.

"This is terrible, Claire. All of it. I don't know if there are people in your life who will be honest or straight with you." She watches him closely, wondering if this is what he looks like when he's sad. She's getting somewhere; at least she won't judge him as quickly as she judged Andrew. *But hadn't I been right to judge him quickly?*

Why did he send the letter? *If only his words hadn't been so beautiful.* If only they hadn't sliced into her, again and again, and especially now, with no one here to tether her, to bring her back to earth. *Always a sucker for beauty.*

...I hear that you're building your little house, deep in the desert.

Luke continues, repeating his desire to help, as though he's nervously reciting a speech he has memorized and practiced too many times. "I'm just saying I want to help you. I have to be straight with you. You just can't stay in that house all day, by yourself. I know it's only been a few days. I know. But I would die if you just rotted away in that house, with nothing to do and no one to see."

That house? she thinks. *Is there something wrong with it? Is it not my house? It's just* that *house? There was bitterness in that letter; he's angry.* She can see that Luke had stopped the letter short of where he wanted. He didn't include the words, but he didn't need to. She knew them already: *You're living for nothing now. I hope you're keeping some kind of record.*

"I know," she says. "I know."

"Do you need to get a job?" he asks.

"I don't think so. Not immediately. But I'm sure eventually." She is shaky on all this.

She was never in charge of the finances, and for good reason, she thought. She knows John had life insurance and they had few debts, but she also knows she'll need to find work to eat. It was one of the first things she thought about after she got the news of John's death. Before the shock really set in, she wondered for a split second how long she'd be able to go without finding a job. She hasn't *needed* a job since she was an undergrad, and even then, she was only working to pay for groceries and extras. Her tuition and some housing costs were covered by her scholarship. She was a promising young scholar. *Was.* There are no more scholarships or promising young scholars. She would never have made it to university then if the current scarcity had been in place. She had been lucky to make it in before the major cut-off. Yes, she will need to get a job. There is no doubt.

"Do you want to stay here? Or do you want to move?" A slight pause. "Maybe it's just too early to say."

Her response is short. "Of course it's too early to say." She looks him straight in the face, meeting his gaze because she knows it will unnerve him, as if to remind him that she is *this Claire*, this particular lost and lonely person, right in front of him, and not some archetypal, theoretical grieving woman. *Fuck him. Fuck the letter.*

It's sappy poetic shit anyhow.

The knotted pit of a realization is slowly rolling down the landscape toward her, and she already knows that she wants to duck out of its way: She will have to figure out how to live the rest of her life. She will have to find work. She will have to meet new people. She will have to recover the strength she once called on to get through every day. She will have to drag herself back out into the world. She will have to inhabit this body.

No one and no thing can live her life on her behalf. *How could I have forgotten this for so many years?*

And what had changed since her youth to make her now afraid of the world, afraid of finding some good places in it? What had she been thinking? That someone could live her life for her? Figure her shit out, look inside her soul, see what she needed, and make it happen? She knew the words but didn't *know* them, clearly: *You shouldn't let other people get your kicks for you.*

Something like purpose is going to have to come from somewhere, she glimpses. From somewhere she can't anticipate. *Job* or *baby* or *husband* will not work. None of it will work. *I am on my own.*

What have I been doing with myself? I am one of the few lucky enough to have food, shelter, and all I can think to do is sit around wishing for a baby?

She has half a mind to order some drinks—lots and lots of drinks—and get terrifically drunk and let Luke seduce her, or to seduce him. To let go of that control she just wrested back as Otis Redding sang to them. *There's no laws or rules to unchain your life.* Why not? Really, why not? She can't say, exactly. Maybe it would take too much effort. She doesn't have much to give him—to give anyone. *I should watch my output*, she realizes.

So when they part ways and Luke gives her a long hug, she lifts her face to him, letting him look at her. She wants to be looked at. But she needs to be careful.

She gives him a deep, forceful kiss, eyes shut tight. She whispers to him, her lips touching his ear: "I see you there with a rose in your teeth." She steps away, turns around to give Luke a half-smile and a little wave, and then she is gone.

Luke stands there as though he's waiting for another friend to arrive, hands in his pockets, shoulders shrugged up. She has said as much as she can. She let him know that she had read the letter after all. She let him know that his cruelty had not gone unnoticed.

But he was right.

You're living for nothing now.

If she had been living for nothing, she had nothing to lose.

TWELVE

She'll arrange her thoughts on a bike ride—look at them like a book that's been pulled apart. Maybe a long bike ride. She'll get some sun, use her legs and her lungs, try not to notice the temperature. *John loved long bike rides.*

Did he ever think it was strange, riding around for hours on a bike in the heat, proudly wasting energy and guzzling water, while everyone else hid from the heat, saved and stored up their energy, their water? Why do we even have bikes?

Pulling her bike from the shed, checking the tires, securing her helmet, she lets herself want and hate him. Luke. She lets herself want Luke. She is remembering how it's easier, and more delicious, to want someone if you haven't acted on the want. It's best to boil from wanting.

Why? Why not? Pain can be productive. This is a manageable, almost pleasurable pain. The other pain—the pain of no more John—is not.

Go toward the pain.

She is aching. Aching because of her wanting. Wanting so badly it aches. This has not happened in years. For a moment she feels young. She recalls this aching with John, before they became John and Claire, Two People in Love. *It was never stronger than it was with John.*

She pushes off, daydreaming as she pedals. Luke comes to get her and he steals her away to Lake Tahoe, to a tiny cabin perched on the lake. Why Lake Tahoe she has no idea. She's never been there, doesn't know if she cares to go there. But he knows a cabin. The air is cool and thin there. *Dream logic doesn't submit to the rules of life.* She will go with it.

Penélopê knew it: *many and many a dream is mere confusion, a cobweb of no consequence at all.*

They arrive at the cabin and spend a day preparing food for each other—windows open—eating together, talking together, talking with the excitement and the fervor of a new couple. They have discovered each other. They have been starved for each other—starved nearly to death— each for the uninterrupted company of the other. They eat and talk, for hours. They watch each other, gaze at each other, they fear taking their eyes off each other. If they could they'd eat each other.

When night falls, it's perfectly chilly and they climb into bed together, but they do not undress. They share sleep without sleeping together. As Claire drifts to sleep in the cabin, Luke runs his fingers along the creases in her palms, committing them to memory. They touch no more than this. Just fingertips on an open palm. He knows that for now this is all he can ask. She knows that for now this is all she can give.

As she rides, Claire can taste the restraint and the longing in that small touch—that committing of her palm to memory—and it twists up her stomach. The smallest touch. Luke's fingers on her open palm. It is too intimate, more intimate than sex could ever be.

She breaks the spell, forcing herself to remember that it's just a daydream. A cobweb of no consequence at all. She keeps pedaling. She is alone. *Everything slips away.*

He won't satisfy her hunger. He never will. *Like everyone else, he'll just get off on watching me starve to death. He can fuck my corpse if that's what he wants. It's what they all want.*

Fuck that letter.

Faster, harder, fuck that letter.

Past that house and that house and that one too, out onto the road that connects hers to a main artery. But she doesn't take this road into town. She lets it lead her away from town, out to the old farmland, now mostly desolate horse properties for people who can handle the heat and love riding and land and their sprawling ranch-style houses.

This heat is dangerous. It hurts. The landscape's shades of yellow and brown and green blur as she rides faster. Small wildflowers on the side of the road reach out to her, tempting her to stop. Eventually, she does.

Should I ride until my body gives out? It wouldn't take long.

Should she throw herself on these train tracks? Should she drink this poison?

She drinks some water. She drinks some more. She picks some wildflowers, clutching them in her clammy hand until she realizes she has no way to bring them home with her. She can't tell how far she's ridden, how long she's been riding, how long it will take her to return to town.

You don't get to sit around dreaming for free. Everything costs something. Sometimes we just don't know that we're paying, or what we're paying for.

She hasn't had to deal with the heat like this in a long time. She hasn't had to face it. Why did she ride this far with only a little water?

Miles from where anyone would find me, she thinks.

Life has been too easy. My life. It has been too easy. It's dangerous.

THIRTEEN

An anchor dropped in her when she met John.

He was just so fully formed. So sure of himself and what he wanted, who he was and could be. Formidable. Not the *formidable* of the French, which she was studying then as her foreign language. He was not nice or sweet. He was alarming. Challenging.

She was so excited by him, by his presence, during their initial courtship, that she was simultaneously too ecstatic to sleep and capable of sleeping more deeply and fully than she ever had before in her adult life. They were drunk on each other, but she was especially tanked. Wasted. Wasting.

Even in the midst of her drunken excitement she knew that she was on the edge of something big, perched on a moment that would shape her life into a series of befores and afters. Before John. After John.

And she knew that if they didn't stay together, couldn't work it out, weren't quite right for each other after all, that After John would be a sad time, that After John would probably feel empty. Instead of pushing the drunkenness away—tipping her into a kind of emotional sobriety—this knowledge heightened her intoxication and made her more vulnerable than she liked to be.

When they first met, she couldn't help laying herself bare for him. She knew the stakes were high with this one, so high that she couldn't pull herself together enough to play any games. She couldn't even flirt with him. All she could do, she realized, was exist side-by-side with him, and if he liked the way she existed, he would want to stick around. Any romantic skill she had learned in her years of casual dating and scrabbling, awkward first relationships were useless. She couldn't play it cool. She wanted John and his incredible strength. And she had no capacity to hide it.

Eventually, though, she perfected her cool. Learned how to curb the vulnerability, how to let John wonder what she was thinking, what she wanted, when she wanted it. She learned how to erect a little wall around her heart.

But why? Why did playing it cool matter? Why did it ever matter? she wonders now. *Self-defense? Self-preservation?* What *self* was there worth defending or preserving if John and his self, so mingled and fused with hers, would eventually be gone?

He had the most beautiful hands. Knotted but also kind of elegant. Seeing his hands reach to touch her skin gave her goose bumps, made her stomach jump. Sometimes he would reach his hands around to the back of her head, to hold her hair back and take in all of her face, and she would feel the need to drop down to her knees. *To pray? As a gesture of supplication? No. Then why?*

Because she simply couldn't stand in the face of the intensity of his love—his desire to just see her, to look at her.

She couldn't have known—wouldn't have believed it— that there would be times in their years together when she would loathe the sight of those same hands reaching for her. That she would reflexively move away from them, the hands that had once seemed to work miracles on the surface of her body.

But this is marriage, isn't it? she thinks. *We take each other for granted.* We have days or years when we want anyone but the husband's hands on us. If we're lucky, we redis-cover those hands, we remember why we needed them. *Until death do us part. If we're not lucky, we submit or get out if we can.*

She knew she had won him fully on the night of their fourth encounter, two weeks into it.

She won him when she figured out how to build the little wall.

She could only have him—they could only have each other—once she determined how to stop laying herself bare. But that's not entirely true. *There was one bare moment. A moment of complete nudity. Maybe it was the nudity that won him after all.* She doesn't know. She can't find John to ask him.

On that night, they drank a little too much at dinner, stayed at the table talking and making each other laugh long after their food had been consumed. It was winter. There was ice on the sidewalks.

They walked out of the restaurant as it closed, into the cold night, and wandered hand-in-hand to the karaoke bar down the street. It was packed. They ordered their bourbons and sat at the only small table available. They shouted over the terrible singers and the crowd singing along.

They kissed and she felt John reaching for her leg under the table. She dissolved a little bit.

She took the big book of songs and the slip of paper on the table, wrote down her selection, and handed the slip of paper to the emcee. She had time to finish another drink before her name was called, so she had enough courage to walk onstage.

John watched her with delight and maybe even a little embarrassment. *Good* she thought. *Let him be a little nervous.* She was drunk and exhilarated. Joy is not far from fear.

Her song began and she jumped in right on time. Her voice wasn't gorgeous but it wasn't terrible either. She held the microphone and sang as strongly as she could, looking straight at John.

Hey little girl is your daddy home? Did he go away and leave you all alone?

He was beaming. Was he also blushing?

The crowd joined her, everyone drunk and singing as loudly as they could. But she held his gaze. *At night I wake up with the sheets soaking wet and a freight train running through the middle of my head.*

He returned her gaze and their eyes stayed locked on each other. *Only you can cool my desire. Ohhhhh I'm on fire.* He was hers. Done.

She hadn't meant to choose a song with such strong sexual overtones. She just liked Bruce Springsteen and knew she wouldn't have to stretch her voice too far to sing along with him.

She was so much more powerful, infinitely more powerful, with the wall up, with John. She felt it later that night, the first time they had sex. If this power had been in her before, she hadn't known it. She'd never felt it boiling under her skin like this before, had never felt murderous with it before. This was part of his magic. When it was over, he kissed her cheeks and held her head, stroking her hair like a father holding his baby.

She couldn't recall anyone being this tender with her, ever. She let the wall fall away, just for a moment. She was engulfed by love. Drowned by it. She was desperate with it. She was nothingness itself in the face of it.

Little speechless tears rolled down her cheeks. People might get hurt—*she* might get hurt—this might fall apart, *but no matter. Let it happen, if it's going to happen. This is worth something* she thought.

"I want to see new places with you. I want to taste new foods with you. I want to live a new life with you." *Reduced to cliché.* She could feel that they would plummet together. They were risking together.

Say it or you'll die: "I want you to undo me. I want you to take me apart."

The disassembly was quick. It only took a moment. And a handful of words he couldn't stop himself from saying, as he sat up and looked at her in awe: "You are knocking me flat."

By the time the wall went back up, she was new. Reconstituted. Restructured. And she had John.

She had never felt an intellectual power before, nor an emotional or a social power, but now she was so full of power she frightened herself. This was the source of a new version of her—built by him, built with him. It was a small, smooth rock of power that she wanted to pluck out of her and slip into her pocket for safekeeping. He was sharing it with her. He conferred power. *So that's what it is to be a man.*

She hadn't seen this coming when they'd first met. She couldn't have known she had this audacity, or this capacity for internal drama.

And she couldn't have known how fleeting it would all be (*What did I do with it?*), and that like all other things, one's sense of self—as powerful or weak or stupid or beautiful—comes and goes as it pleases.

FOURTEEN

Come find me.

She returns from the bike ride with no sense of how long she's been gone. She stumbles inside, the skin of her shoulders and arms aching, burning. The sun is starting to set, the desiccation is more bearable. Was it midday when she left? Early afternoon?

She puts her face under the kitchen faucet, drinking the water in greedy gulps, letting it run down her cheeks and onto her hair, the neckline of her shirt. She turns the water off and wonders, as she sometimes does, if it will turn on the next time she opens the tap.

———

She has so much correspondence—so many *condolences*—

waiting for her. She'll pick through it and decide what to respond to now, what to avoid.

An email from the bank has a serious and official tone, referencing the times they've tried and failed to reach her. Can she come to the bank first thing tomorrow morning for a meeting with their personal banker? With a little bit of fear building in her stomach, she responds and says that yes, she will come to the bank first thing tomorrow morning. She didn't know she and John *had* a banker.

She needs some food. Does she want company? Should she find an empty spot at a bar, make small talk with the bartender? She'll leave now. See what she sees.

She drives through this town, this place where she once did some growing up and that once felt so special, but now is just any other place to her. *Any other place where people live and die, fight and fuck, eat and shit.*

She drives slowly.

She passes the park where in high school her fast friend Chrissy told an ancient craggy-faced Vietnam vet she'd give him a blow job if he bought the two of them some beer. She passes all those benches on bustling street corners where she sat with friends for hours of mindless girlfriend chatter, where she held hands with boys she thought she loved, where she sometimes sat by herself, learning how to be alone without feeling lonely. She passes the grocery store where she accompanied her mother on countless shopping trips. She passes the gas station where she used her first fake ID to buy cigarettes and cheap wine.

She pulls into the driveway of her parents' old house,

nestled among the tall pines and the other modest homes tucked back among the trees, barely visible from the road.

They left years ago, her parents, before she and John moved here, so there's no hope of seeing them emerge from the front doors, waving and smiling. And she doesn't know if she'd like to see them now anyway; there's been only one short phone call since the news of John's death. They "couldn't make it" to the funeral. They are not what anyone would call caring or attentive or even *present* parents.

Nonetheless, she's drawn to this driveway like a fool. She hasn't come here since she and John moved to this town. She's not sure why. *Odd. I used to live here.*

There must be someone here who can save me.

A few lights are on, but it doesn't seem as though anyone is home. There's no happy familial scene for her to watch from the driveway. No one gathering round the table. No one calling the kids down from their rooms, telling them to wash up. No one pouring a glass of wine. No one pulling the roast from the oven.

Yes, I need company, she realizes. She needs company or else. Or else what? *Or else what?*

It doesn't matter. She picks up her phone and calls Luke. She doesn't know if they should see each other. But she needs her friend.

He answers after two rings. Calmly, "Claire. How are you?"

"You wanna get dinner?"

"Yes," he says. "As long as you don't have other obligations."

"I'm not sure if I do," she says, knowing what they are, knowing she can't face them yet. "Where should we meet?"

They pick a place and arrange to meet there in fifteen minutes.

She'll drive slowly. *God this heat* she thinks as she starts the car again and turns on the air conditioning. The rains should start soon. Any moment now. The ground is aching for it.

Or maybe the rains will stop coming. Maybe that's how they'll all go—wandering in the desert, searching for an oasis, collapsing under the weight of their stupidity.

When she sees him at the restaurant she immediately regrets calling him.

What's that look in his face? A mixture of sadness, pity, and disappointment. *No. None of that.* She can't stand anymore of his *you deserve better, please be nice to yourself* bullshit.

Did he talk to Andrew? Would Andrew have told him?

She can see him clearly now, right now, tonight. This is not the Luke she knew as an undergrad. Not the Luke she's known as a man tied down by responsibilities he wasn't sure he wanted. Not even the Luke she saw earlier at the diner. He has changed.

She will try to eat, try to talk. She will push past the regret.

She orders a burger and when it arrives, she is dumbstruck. The sumptuousness of it, the luxury of it. *The kind of meal I may one day dream about.* The perfect stack of the burger, so much opulence held together with just a toothpick. The little mountain of fries, soaked in salt and fat, crispy, radiating abundance. *This is unbelievable.*

She eats and finds that her hunger keeps coming. She is eating so quickly that she has to force herself to talk to Luke, to slow down the consumption.

It is not the talking and the eating and the consuming of each other of her waking dream on the bike. The dream was just a dream—nothing more. They probably can't consume each other, she sees, and still live their lives. *Live with the hunger.*

Luke reports that he has gone to see John's parents. They were glad to see him, but they are not well. No one would be surprised. He says he plans to keep checking in on them, that they shouldn't be alone every day.

She had forgotten how his casual intelligence was disarming. He has something to say about everything, but he does not hold forth. He asks questions, he is interested. He can be charming, without knowing it.

She orders a second burger. "Did John ever tell you," she asks, "that I wanted to have a baby?"

"No," he responds, with a note of surprise. "I guess I figured it would eventually happen, but I imagined he would want a baby more than you."

"He would want a baby more than me? Before I wanted

one?" Her voice sounds strange to her. She has been silent for so many days.

"I guess." He shrugs. "It seemed like the next step for him, for both of you. You'd be good parents. It's not easy though, and I worry a lot about what, what—"

"What their futures might be?"

"Something like that. If they'll make it. There's no certainty for them. I don't like thinking about it."

She sees the concern in his face. She remembers one month last year when she thought she might be pregnant, and how she found herself awake in the night, certain they had made a mistake. Anxiety swallowed her whole. There was no water, there was no food. What if the bottom really fell out and there were no jobs for them and their meager savings couldn't go very far? What would they do? Two days later her period arrived and the concern dissolved.

"I understand. I really wanted a baby, despite all that," she says. "I can't explain it." She pauses. "We tried for a long time."

He is silent in response. He wants to reach across the table and take her hand, but he doesn't.

"I wanted other things too, I think. I want more than just a baby. But still," her voice trails off.

He knows she has romanticized parenthood and that she has little idea what it really requires. He doesn't tell her this. He doesn't want to prove that he knows something she doesn't. He doesn't want to change her mind. He wants to be here with her.

They are talking about John, because they can't stop themselves, because he is the reason they're at this table together.

"You know what I already miss most about him?" Luke says.

His eyes are beautiful. "What?"

"His loud laugh." Luke stops to think. "No wait. His ubiquity. He was always there. Everyone could count on him. Always. It's a special quality in a person."

She had forgotten how thoughtful he is. *There's something exquisite buried in him. I should be better to him.*

She isn't sure how to respond. "No one could accuse him of being irresponsible. Or indifferent." *Is it true?*

"You don't think he was always available? Always *there*?" Sensing that he might be on too-sensitive ground, he pauses. "Is it okay to talk about this? Are you okay with it?" There's a solidity to him she hadn't noticed before. *Was I ever that solid?*

She can't say. Right now she's a boat being built at sea, plank by plank, but it doesn't seem to be working. *As soon as two planks come together, two others pull apart.*

"I'm okay with it," she says. Then, after a pause, "What is shock?"

"I don't know," he says.

They hug goodbye when they part ways. It is a calm, cautious hug. As though neither of them could stomach reliving the drama of their last encounter. They have gotten ahold of themselves.

Red night sky, heat soaring up from the concrete. The parking lot is empty. A bag of trash is caught between two electrical wires above her head. They are pulled taut, and the bag is almost resting atop them as if on a platter. She laughs to herself.

FIFTEEN

She arrives for the banking appointment the next day with a knot in her stomach.

She doesn't want to know what the bank has to tell her. That she has no money? That John had no money? God knows she can't ask her parents for help. John's parents, yes, but she knows they're saving everything they can, being too old to reliably find work.

Her family had always hovered just above poverty, so she wasn't afraid of being booted out of the middle class or whatever existed of it, the way her friends whose parents had money were. But still, she had been close enough to poverty to know it held no romance, no mystique.

Could she work her way back into the industry she left so swiftly, happily, certain she was moving up to house-wifery and motherhood? Would she have to start again, get an entry-level job, earn the kind of paycheck that could maybe cover groceries? Or would she have to move further south, to one of the sweltering camping colonies, like so many others?

Claire walks unsteadily in to the bank and introduces herself to the first attentive person. With an "Oh yes" she is led to a desk at the rear of the large, open room. No private cubicle. No room with a closing door. *Is this a good sign?* A smartly dressed young woman introduces herself to Claire with a surprising amount of confidence.

"I won't take up too much of your time," the banker says.

"I have a lot of time."

A nervous chuckle is covered with a polite smile. "Of course." A long pause, and Claire offers nothing to fill it. "Well," the banker begins, "there are just a few forms we need you to sign."

Claire's confusion is visible, and the banker is not prepared for what she has to say next. "Ma'am, since your husband has, uhhhh, passed," her voice nearly cracking, "his accounts not already shared with you are to be transferred to you, and we need to know where you want those funds."

"Which funds?" Claire asks. "And why wouldn't they just go into the checking account or the regular savings account?" Her confusion is ramping up.

"Your husband had a trust, mostly untouched, and the funds are to be transferred to the accounts you two shared. They can of course go into your checking or regular savings account, as you've mentioned. Or they can be split up, for instance if you'd like some to go into the savings account, opened…" rifling through papers, she finds the date she seeks, "two weeks ago. Or if you'd like the money to do some work for you, there are higher-yield options." She concludes, sounding vaguely satisfied. But looking up, the banker can see in Claire's face that she knew nothing of this.

Clearly terrified, the banker drops the formality. With a deep breath and a lowered voice, aiming for woman-to-woman closeness, she says, "I helped your husband open a new account the other week. He told me about the baby, and he wanted to start a savings account immediately. Congratulations, by the way." She had tried, at least, to end on a happy note.

"But, but, I'm not pregnant," Claire says, knitting her brows so tight they're practically touching in the middle. "I'm not, I haven't, I, I'm not...pregnant." There's a long pause.

"Oh my god I'm so sorry," the banker says. Her mortification is total. Her hands are shaking as she first covers her mouth and then begins to reach across the desk to touch Claire. She stops short of Claire's hand.

Speaking quickly, trying to think on her feet, Claire says, "Well... I... maybe it was an account for a theoretical baby, or a baby in the future I mean, but I, I'm not pregnant."

"Oh god. I am so so very sorry," the banker begs. "Yes, that's it. I wasn't remembering our conversation clearly. Until now. Yes, he just said he was getting ready to start a family. He never said a baby was actually on the way. I am so, just so..." and she trails off, her face the deepest cerise.

Claire is still. She isn't sure what to say.

"He seemed really happy!" the banker continues. "He did. He seemed really happy!" She was new to the job but smart enough to know that this couldn't possibly be a consolation. She will remember this interaction for the rest of her life.

A rock materializes in Claire's throat. She leaves as quickly as she can, signing the necessary papers in a dazed rush, hoping she doesn't throw up on the way out. It was only a few thousand dollars; why had they dragged her through this? Why had *he* dragged her through this?

Could John have been stupid enough to think a baby would just show up *after years of trying, with no success? What the fuck?* Had he made appointments to begin pursuing IVF or something equally aggressive without her? *Why wouldn't he have told me? What had he been thinking? What the fuck was his problem?*

The specifics didn't matter, she realized, with a sadness —and a deep, limitless longing—dropping on her, burrowing all the way into her.

What mattered is that John had wanted a baby and had planned for one. *Maybe he had heard me. Maybe everything didn't have to be on his terms.*

Maybe they hadn't been so far apart after all. They would have been imperfect parents, but they could have been parents, together. They would not have known what they were doing, they would not have known how to do it together, but they would have tried.

Maybe she hadn't been as dutiful as she thought. Maybe she had just been patient.

Realizing all of this felt to her like those times as a young child when she'd overhear someone saying something unflattering or unkind about her mother. A terrifying moment of understanding that her world is not *the* world. But didn't everyone understand that her mother was the sun and the moon, cruel as she was? Didn't everyone dream of having her long legs? Could Claire have been *wrong* to need her as fiercely as she did? Was the world as mean and petty as those whispering gossips made it seem?

She returns to the car and buckles herself in. She's collapsing in on herself. She can't bear this. Her body can't contain this much fear and regret and sadness. The bubble of heat in the car is so intense that she screams.

She screams again. Her face is red, little beads of sweat are forming on her forehead, her hands are shaking.

I don't want to let you go. I don't want to let you go!

To him. To this version of herself that was *with* him. *But mostly to him.*

As though he could hear her, reach for her with his hands and say, *You don't have to, Cee. I'm here.* As though anyone could hear her.

Her head hits the steering wheel and she brings her hands to her face, hiding her tears from the world. *But we were still just beginning*, she thinks.

Sometimes people can walk away with the best parts of you—or any parts of you—tucked safely under their arms. You can keep looking for those parts but you'll never find them. They are not where you left them.

Such a deep pain. Such a strong, flexible pain. Reaching for every part of her.

She sits for a minute, letting the tears drip onto the knees of her jeans. She sucks in as much air as she can and starts the car.

SIXTEEN

As the day rolls into the afternoon, the first monsoon arrives. It is merciful. The sun disappears and the rain falls hard enough to hurt, to pierce flesh.

The sky is cracking open, thick layers of clouds separating to let knife-blades of sunshine through, rain falling so hard it fills the washes in great gusts. The warm, wet smell of creosote rising up from the desert floor. Birds go silent as it falls in sheets, then they cheer to one another as it stops and their meals are pushed up to the surface of the earth.

It has always been this beautiful when the rain finally comes.

The landscape dark and ominous, calling Claire to drive to the end of it, to see if she will sail right off the edge of the earth, to see if those rain-drenched mountains will swallow her.

The rain will bring thirty minutes or so of relief from the heat. She could get a good start, driving with the windows down, feeling the fresh air.

Instead she pulls over and sits in silence, listening to the rain. Gushes of it pour over the windshield, as though someone were standing on the roof, crazily emptying buckets of water onto the car. She watches a bird in a tree. Its figure keeps getting obscured by the streams of rain on the windows. It looks so still. *Are we doing the same thing?* It isn't making a sound.

John's mother calls her, for maybe the fifth time since yesterday, but she lets it go to voicemail. With his mother she will have to perform Loving Wife, and she does not have it in her.

She lets herself fall back into bed, feeling that ache we feel when we know our incompleteness. The incompleteness that strikes us, lands as a thud in our chests.

A thudding, relentless sorrow. The projects begun and never finished—the projects never begun that could have been perfect. The half-hearted attempts at painting, the friendships that dangled, uncertain and mostly uninteresting. The dreams, the compulsions, the desires, the unfinished—*unfinishable*—shit of being a human with never enough time to complete the project of being human.

Live with the hunger. You will never be full.

This incompleteness stalks her these days, presenting as a low-level melancholy, compelling her to sleep or sleepwalk through the day, to forget the thousand or so little things and the couple hundred big things she hasn't done, will never do, will never see her husband do. The things she can't bear to say she'll do *in his place* or *because he'd want me to.*

What would he want me to do? How could I ever know?

It's not just him she misses; it's herself, too. *Whatever kind of love we had, it killed us. It killed both of us.* This is what her life has cost her.

SEVENTEEN

Why is John worth mourning? What did he and Claire have that was special? *Everything. Nothing.* They just clicked. How boring to admit it. They simply fit into each other's lives well.

And for an unknowable constellation of reasons, they were able to keep fitting into each other's lives as they turned from young adults into adults, and as they approached middle age. They were supposed to be together. Everything in their lives dictated that they each find a suitable partner, that they remained partnered at all costs.

Did we "settle" for each other? The dreaded settling. As though the fiery passion that has, say, two star-crossed impulsive Italian teenagers dying for each other were sustainable, or even desirable. As though romance was only about feverish fucking and not about doing the dishes even though you don't want to, because your husband is sick and needs to get to bed early.

Did we "work" on us, on our marriage? As though maintaining one of the most important relationships of one's life were comparable to what so many of us call work: answering emails, sitting in meetings, submitting reports, traveling to meetings, wrangling young bodies and brains in various educational institutions, making food, cleaning floors and toilets, installing ovens and fridges, tele-video-conferencing, day in and day out. Or for the rest, the work of staying alive is the whole of it. Finding food, finding shelter.

What even is "work" now? It feels like a lifetime since she had a job—since she "worked." *"What do people do?" wondered Daisy Buchanan,* she remembers. *But Daisy's life was so much work.*

Is she just some twenty-first century equivalent of Daisy? A lot less money but just as lonely, just as foolish, just as discarded by men who use her to feel their strength and power and then walk away? Is she just like the rest of them? *Just as unhappy to be nothing more than a pretty fool, submitting instead of committing suicide? Poor Daisy. Poor all of them. Created by men.*

She lets herself follow the thread. It's too painful to follow, but maybe it will be worth it. There is no redemptive power in suffering. *But.*

Face the suffering, suffer a little more in facing it, she can see, and maybe you can learn how to avoid it. How painful is this thread—how many others are linked to it? Will pulling on it unravel the entire sweater?

John did not discard me, but did he respect her? Did he? Pulling on the thread means facing the distinct possibility that she has never in her life known a man who respected her. Plenty have liked her, loved her, wanted her, dreamed of her, brought her gifts, made her offers and promises, been kind and gentle with her, but had any of them ever respected her? The older ones, the younger ones, the smarter ones, the dumber ones, any of them?

Did any of them respect Pénelopê? Or Ophelia or Juliet or the Virgin Suicides girls or or...

Not the ones who reached their greedy proprietary hands for the small of her back as they led her out the door. Not the ones who cooly took her in and then let their eyes glaze over in boredom at every word she spoke after they learned that she was the property of another man. Not the ones who cursed her for not wanting to fuck them, on their terms, on their timeline, according to their desires—desires that they felt entitled to share with her, to foist on her. Not, even, the ones who treated her as something sacred and fragile— the ones who needed her to baptize them with her body. *How lonely,* she realizes. *How lonely to be unrespectable.*

...or or Anna or even worse, the ones who weren't even visible, the slave girls, the attendant girls, the domestic helper girls, the rape victims and the ones stabbed to death to make it real and gritty—the ghosts that haunt everything she thought she loved.

Claire could never understand—she always felt five steps behind. What was she not learning? What could she not intuit? She had tried her hardest, always, but she kept running up against the fact that no matter how hard she tried—to be smart, to be kind, to be beautiful, to be interesting—she was already marked to most as unworthy of respect. Now she can see it. *She had been trying to earn something she could never earn. Never.*

Her marriage was a work contract, the penalties too great for her to entertain violating the unspoken terms of the agreement. Everything costs something. Who benefits from the terms being unspoken? *How many of them are unspoken?*

Daisy and all the others knew they would bear the burden if the terms were violated.

―――――

Why did the encounter in the bank hurt so much? Because it might be evidence that John had respected her. What is respect if not the willingness to at least try to do something you're not sure you can do, for the sake of someone else? *You can love and respect someone even if you're caught up in something you don't want to be caught up in, even if you don't know you're caught up in it.*

Why is John worth mourning? He and his respect are gone.

I'll have to start all over again.

EIGHTEEN

Go toward the pain.

She has lived here before. She knows this place, but it is still strange to her. *I am still a stranger here.*

She and her sister and her parents moved here when she was nearly a teenager, and her parents stayed until Claire and Dacia, much younger than Claire, finished high school. John had visited only once by the time they decided to move here. Claire's family no longer lived here, but they had provided a reason to visit years ago, when Dacia threw herself a high school graduation party. John was not a stranger to the landscape, to the extreme climate that had only grown more extreme, to the stubborn inoperability of the desert, but it wasn't home for him, as it was for Claire.

When she and John moved to this small town, they

arrived as a couple, as adults, as people with at least a little experience in the world. But the moment she stepped foot into their lovely little rental home she felt seventeen again.

The first few weeks she was up at night with memories of this place she'd forgotten fifteen years ago. The way the ground was so dusty that in the spring, when the rains were far away, all her shoes would turn the same light brown color. Memories of standing around outside her high school kicking at the dirt, watching little clouds of it swirl up and settle back down. How at night her nose would crack from the dryness and she'd have to excavate dry little bloody boogers all day.

How once the water started going, only the richest and most resourceful and most desperate stayed. How the ranchers would come into town in their worn-out Carhartts and their hats and boots and spend a week's pay at the bars downtown, ready to buy anyone a drink. Once she and a friend snuck in to one of these bars before they were 21 and she let a sad drunk ranch-hand hold her on the dancefloor while Garth Brooks sang about domestic violence. She'd felt ashamed of how clean her clothes were. *There are only a few ranchers left.*

John's experience went far here; his pay and the low cost of living meant they could rent a house with more space than they were accustomed to. The landlord lived many towns away and told them they could do what they liked to the house, so long as they paid rent. In this small town, they would not have to struggle to make rent. Even more reason for Claire to think less and less about finding her way back into the job she'd so hurriedly left.

They hadn't even been here for three years when John died.

John's parents weren't far away—a two-hour drive northwest, through an endless string of towns positioned awkwardly, haphazardly around the small highway—towns that gave—and for Claire will always give—reason to pause.

Trailer parks, lean-tos, convenience stores, roving bands of sunburned kids. The skinny, malnourished guys with their fat, pregnant wives, pushing beat-up strollers along the highway in full sun—strollers already stuffed with babies. Their eyes vacant and shifty, their faces pocked with meth blisters. Roadside jerky and salsa stands, packs of day laborers waiting by the side of the road to be picked up for jobs that don't exist, the odd dead coyote or skunk, *road kill has its seasons just like everything.* All in the middle of a natural beauty so arresting it makes her eyes ache.

It made sense to be here. It didn't matter that Claire's family was no longer here; in fact it was better—probably much better—that she and John could land here on their own terms, alone together. She knew this place, or remembered it, and wanted to know it freshly, newly.

They settled in. Became regulars at the bars they liked, tipped and befriended the servers at the two restaurants they frequented, figured out their favorite walks, the streets with the nicest houses they could peek into, with lives they could eavesdrop on. They made new friends, got back in touch with all the old friends scattered around the region. Andrew was nearby; they spent a lot of time together, the three of them laughing and getting stoned. They were lucky and stupid.

John was happy here. Claire could tell. He thrived in this new job, feeling secure with some big city work experience already under his belt, his parents close, a social life almost ready-made for them. He was thrilled to have a house to tend to. No more shoebox apartments with only views of other shoebox apartments. Claire was surprised to see how proud he was of this house that wasn't even his.

He became handy in ways he'd once scoffed at. John invited his dad to make the drive to the house almost every weekend, and his dad happily arrived early on Saturday mornings with a thermos of coffee, overjoyed to spend his free time teaching his son how to build a table, fix a leaky faucet, re-tile a bathroom, extend the back deck.

It wasn't long before Claire admitted that she wanted to have a baby. At first it was casual. She would bring it up, but she was careful not to pressure John or make him uncomfortable, so the conversation took the tone of *Maybe we should try for a baby sometime soon*. John was in total agreement, or so he thought: sometime soon, but not right now.

He didn't realize that he was setting the terms, but he was.

He didn't understand that Claire's forced casualness was bait he hadn't taken. She figured she would be casual about it and he would be enthusiastic—as with most things—and so he would think the idea had been his. He needed to think the ideas were his.

And mostly they were. In this way they were no different than many generations of married couples before them. Claire's younger, more scholarly self might have assertively wondered if there were any clearer example of male privilege than a man unknowingly and casually setting the terms for when and how a woman would carry a baby. That younger version might have seen a red flag the moment Claire decided that she couldn't be honest with John, that she felt the need to play a game she probably couldn't win. But this version of Claire was growing desperate. She didn't like it. She didn't know what to do about it. She couldn't force the desire to be a mother out of her. She couldn't expel it.

A few times she fantasized about leaving him. She wouldn't need a baby if she didn't have a man—it wouldn't even be a question. She wouldn't need a man if she had something she wanted to do with her life. The sickly logic of depression: *love* and what might be good about it doesn't factor in most of the time.

But here she was, in the middle of the desert. *Where would I go?* Would she dare go *to* anyone else? She couldn't abandon John.

She knew she was fully faithful to him when Luke's post-divorce letter to her arrived, saturated by longing for her, dripping with regret at having missed his chance many years ago. If she went to Luke, even for a night, she would come back to John as nobody's wife. She couldn't do it.

The letter. If there had ever been a time to cut bait and go, that was it. Without being able to articulate it, she could see when the letter came that she only knew herself with John. She knew that she had created herself with him— and that he had played such a large role as her co-creator —that to break away and re-create herself would be a monumental undertaking.

She might rather die than do it. She wasn't sure.

But the fact was that there had never been a place for her, with a man or without. Never was a place for her. Never would be.

Not a single place was for her or any other woman. No safe place. No good place. No secure place. Nothing approaching security. No place for any woman on this planet, ever. What we call melodrama is the honesty we can no longer hide from, when we're worn down to nearly nothing.

What had she been looking for? Had she found it? Had she ever had anything to lose?

Locked into her role as wife, the Baby Conversations became sharper, toothier, the stakes exponentially higher. Claire's tone shifted from casual to casually strained to tense and anxious. She was afraid they would never recover the magic of their first years together. She was afraid that she might actually be as worthless as the world had suggested. She would dissolve fully into marriage, whatever it was, if a new variable wasn't introduced.

John had seen this developing but didn't know what to do about it. *Goddamit Claire*, he would find himself saying. *I can't just make myself ready for something as big as parenthood just because you don't know what to do with yourself.*

She knew he pitied her. She knew he thought her self-indulgent, lazy, pathetic. *We have so much more than most* he'd say. *Can't you just be satisfied?*

They were cruel things to say, he knew. He could see the pain they caused her. He had been the one to suggest quitting her job, and he encouraged her to do it, after all, when she had waffled. He liked the idea of being the sole provider, feeling important in a way that was new to him. And what was the point of both of them working when she made so much less than him and hated her job anyway?

The rivers of shit that flow from your mouth, she had wanted to say.

What he hadn't understood at the time, he could eventually see with some distance, is that Claire's job had given her headaches, but it had also given her somewhere to be each day, a reason to get up and get dressed, people to talk to, no matter how much she hated the job. It should not have surprised him that she had a feverish desire to have a baby the moment joblessness stopped being an exciting change. She wasn't going to home-make. It wasn't her. She had no projects, no crafts, no hobbies to give herself to. She had only a few friends. And there were few women her age in this small town who didn't work and didn't have children to care for. She was alone.

The dangerous overdetermined quality of the thing called family. She can see it now. *We're not supposed to want or need anyone else.*

He hated her for these things, and he had made them happen. What he couldn't look deeply enough to see —and what Claire would only discover with time—is that it wasn't just about a baby. It's never *just about a baby* or *having something to do*. It was that when the job vanished, too much of her agency went with it. She was in danger of disappearing. The only acceptable form of agency for a woman of her age, in this place, in this time, was tied directly to a job or, even better, motherhood. The pressure of this fact had changed her, re-shaped her. It shouldn't have. It did anyway.

Once they almost had it out—almost had the fight they needed to have. In one still moment, she had embraced him, desperate for touch, for John to push her back into herself, to keep her from escaping. She looked at him, letting the fear show in her eyes. *Help*, she wanted to say. *Can you see?*

"There's too much that's unsayable," John said. "You say what you need to say in a situation like this, and you're an asshole no matter what."

And words were not really his strong point to begin with. It seemed to Claire that he was at risk of saying the wrong thing—or saying the right thing the wrong way—

when he wasn't even sure that what he needed to say even *could* be said.

And what did Claire think he wanted or needed to say?

I don't know if I know or like myself. How can I shape another self? No, not quite.

I am good at telling people what to do and pretending like I mean it, but mostly I just follow orders? Closer, maybe.

If you are lonely, if we are lonely, I don't think a baby can fix that? Closer still.

Claire knew that babies don't fix relationships, but she couldn't help but suspect that babies could fix loneliness. *And they do sometimes, don't they? A baby can love you—and help you love—in ways a husband or partner couldn't possibly approach, can't it?*

Of course John wanted to be a father, to have a baby, he said. He had always been clear about that. But he had imagined more time without a baby. Time. Always more time. Couldn't they wait until they were 35, 36, 40? Why now, when they had just barely settled in here, when they still had youth to burn?

Because Claire felt useless is why. John didn't know first-hand how dangerous that could be, but he sensed it. Claire was not her charming, smart, and sexy self with nothing to do, nothing other than domesticity. Maybe motherhood would restore those things to her? Or maybe it would push her further into this depression or whatever it was that had her so baby-obsessed.

In any case, as Claire's father-in-law would later tell her, John saw that he had to do something. His father was not a man of many words, but he would help, offer perspective that John couldn't yet have at his age. His father would know what to do.

And indeed he did. He told John, in so many words: You're waiting for nothing. You're waiting because you're afraid and you're still a child yourself. Grow up. If you know you want to, have that baby or those babies while you hopefully can. Listen to your wife if she tells you she's unhappy. Get yourself to the doctor, get everything checked out, and then start a savings account for that kid pronto. Even if they happen naturally, kids don't come cheap these days. Who cares if the world is ending? It has always been ending.

The wisdom of that generation that can see *considering complexity* for what it sometimes is: fear to do anything whatsoever. A kind of paralysis.

So John did as his father said—making appointments for himself at two separate fertility clinics, opening a savings account—just weeks before he died. He was not the only one here, he could see.

———

They loved each other. *We had love.*

And they had mutual respect. She wasn't sure if it mattered that their respect was flawed and leaning toward patriarchal. *What isn't?* They had a genuine desire to please each other most of the time. They had the shared dream of being together. They were not perfectly selfless. But they were mostly good to each other, mostly good *for* each other. They wouldn't have a chance to learn how to fit together more perfectly.

A baby would not have fixed the uselessness, the loneliness, but a baby would have been more love.

Love is worth it.

But John is gone. Gone and gone and gone.

She is still here.

NINETEEN

It's the afternoon now and a friend from high school, Rebecca, is picking her up. Rebecca has come into town for the funeral. She's going to offer practical help; this is what Rebecca does.

She picks Claire up, and together they drive to the store to get ingredients for meals they'll make and freeze, to keep Claire going. The sort of thing one does for friends with newborn babies. It's almost old-world now. Rebecca lives in the Bay Area, and like someone who's lived in New York, she won't let you forget this fact. It's now a defining feature of her adult personality. The One Who Made it in a Big, Overpriced City and Now Has the Authority to Scoff at the Place She Came From.

On the way to the store, looking out the window, Rebecca says, "This place is fucking depressing."

"I guess," Claire responds, not turning to look at Rebecca as she speaks.

"It's just a string of meth labs. Was it always like this?"

Rebecca asks half-rhetorically. She says, "All these trailer parks and shithole houses," as though this were her first time visiting.

"I think the poor areas are pretty concentrated," Claire says with a note of defensiveness. "There are just as many rich people here as poor people. What should the city do? Move the poor people out? Evict them and raze their shitty houses? Find a way to just give them all jobs? Tell capitalism to move back in?"

The mostly comfortable silence of friends bickering like siblings sets in. Rain starts to fall slowly. They pass a group of boys on their skateboards. A little pack of wolves edging into the street from the sidewalk, warning that the street is sometimes their territory too.

Rebecca's eyes linger on the boys as she turns to Claire and asks, "Were you in high school when you lost your virginity? Is that something an old friend should know?" with a little laugh. "When was it?"

"You mean like when was the exact moment?" Claire asks, with her own little laugh. The boys are in the rearview mirror now, shouting happily at each other, pushing their hair out of their eyes. They look so small.

"Yes," Rebecca says. "The moment when you lost your virginity. Had sex. C'mon."

Feeling strangely puzzled by the question, Claire responds, "But it wasn't just one moment. It was, well, continuous. For most of high school and the beginning of college."

"You know what I mean, Claire. When did you first have sex?"

"Do you mean like penis-in-vagina sex? Oral sex? The first time I made out with a guy and let him take off my bra?"

"Jesus, you know exactly what I mean. I can tell you I was seventeen and it was with David and it was not great."

Claire can feel some of her mental acuity returning, as though she were slowly waking up. Dinner with Luke sobered her up last night.

But she's not sure she can answer Rebecca. Not clearly. Because by the time she had Sex sex, it wasn't very significant. Or maybe it was. But it was just another sexual thing to happen in a long, steady process of *becoming* sexual. Figuring out how to be a sexual being. The first moment of Sex sex was not a big deal compared to the first kiss, the first time a guy went down on her. *Those* were virginity-losing moments. There were many of them. She's surprised by her clarity on the matter. It takes years of shitty Sex sex to finally have good sex. Holding hands and making out on a park bench was better than all those first times combined.

Watching Claire think, Rebecca asks, "Okay, fine, but who did you lose your virginity *to?*"

"Three or four different guys, I guess."

Quickly seizing the opportunity to make Claire laugh, Rebecca says, "Oooh alright! All at once? Standard college-orientation orgy?"

Laughing at herself (god it felt good; she had forgotten that she had a sense of humor), at how she'd opened this door, Claire says, "Actually that sounds like no fun at all.

But no, not an orgy. Three or four different guys who introduced me to sex, I guess."

"So no one forced himself on you and just, like, made it happen?"

"No." *But.*

What *had* happened at the dawn of her sexuality? In truth, she knows, it wasn't as smooth or linear or painless as she makes it sound.

She had mostly lost her virginity—all kinds of physical virginity and her *conceptual* virginity—to one person. The slightly older guy. Impossibly sexy. A wannabe poet. *Oh god, am I still as pathetic, as clueless now as I was then?*

They had met through mutual friends. He was the townie who was too beautiful to be called a townie. His commitment to the work of appearing to be the half-stoned vagabond for beauty, day in and day out, was astonishing. Women more or less lined up to fuck him. Claire was terrified of him.

As a high-schooler, Claire was not one of the pretty girls, not really even one of the popular girls, so she had no idea what to do with herself when *He* seemed to notice her, to take her in with a long gaze and offer a devilish half-smile. She was not accustomed to such attention. One tiny flicker of attraction, of *acknowledgement*, from him and she was struck dumb. She would be sunk by him, she knew it. She couldn't have cared less.

When she looks at photos of herself from high school, she understands why he noticed her. She was not cute or adorable in the way of the pretty and popular girls, but you could see that she would eventually—maybe even shortly—be beautiful. Not cute, not adorable, but beautiful, in time. A beautiful woman.

She wonders sometimes how different her life might be if she hadn't skipped *cute* or *adorable* and gone awkwardly into *beautiful* after some time being neither here nor there. *Would I have stayed in this town forever? Settled down with one of the stupid boys I hated myself for finding attractive in high school?*

He. She still doesn't like to say his name, doesn't want to particularize him. Thank god she has no photos of him, that he exists nowhere on social media. Let him remain universal—the cloud of walking sex and barely instantiated splendor—that he was to her back then.

She watched him. Studied him. Drank in his posture, his gestures, his turns of phrase every time she saw him—at parties, at the coffee shop, wandering aimlessly downtown.

She had never seen someone so confident spending so much time in public alone. He sat at the café with a book and a pen and some loose pieces of paper—just before the days of laptop ubiquity—composing his little lines, the center of this tiny world, an ocean in lithe, dark-eyed human form.

He sat down across from her at the coffee shop one day, one hot afternoon at the end of her junior year, as she waited for her drink and her friend waited for the bathroom.

"Hey," he said casually. And she, drawing on a reserve of

nonchalance she didn't know existed, responded with an equally casual "Hey."

Within a week, she was in his car, listening to Purple Rain and making out with a promising ferocity. His skilled hands and fingers. Good god his hands. His mouth that tasted of tobacco and beer. His lips against her ear: Her first drug. All of it her first serious high.

There is one night that stands out.

He was leaving. Finally leaving this shithole, and he wanted to spend a night with her. Despite, or maybe because of his comprehensive sexual experience, he hadn't pressured her for anything she wasn't ready for.

He had always watched her carefully, not wanting to push her too far and to push her away. Later she realized this was likely because he was getting it elsewhere, anywhere really, all the time, anytime. He was mostly tender with her, but it was incidental tenderness. It wasn't *for* her, he wasn't *loving*; he could afford to be patient with her.

But on this night he is stoned. Stoned enough that he can't watch her, or himself, closely, or at all. It's one of his last nights in town, he reminds her.

Maybe he has plans with different girls and women for each of his last nights in town, but she doesn't care. On this night they've drunk their beers in her parents' car, smoked some weed in the shed behind his dad's house, wandered with clasped hands to the few open places in town. A grimy pool hall, the kind of rural bar she'll eventually come to love and fear in equal measure, the convenience store attached to a gas station where he bums cigarettes from the girls who work behind the counter.

She knows there's nowhere else for them to go. They could do it in the car she borrowed from her parents, or they could do it in his dad's house—if his dad's not home —or they could do it out in the desert next to some scrub oaks and boulders. It wasn't so hot then. They could wander outside for hours without fear of heat stroke.

The paradoxical and paralyzing fact of being in a rural town so small: The land stretches forever outside this town, but the town is small enough that privacy is unachievable.

But none of this is on her mind then. This is the night of her first real sexual encounter and she can feel it coming. It's like sensing the presence of another breathing creature in a darkened room. She knows it's there, but she doesn't know what it is. The fear and exhilaration intensify each other.

He must have known that the shrine was the only place likely to be empty in the middle of the night. St. Joseph is at the foot of the hill. The shrine winds up through the hill. She can see the cross at the top, the white ceramic Jesus glowing a little in the moonlight. He lights the candles at the shrine, slowly, carefully, taking his time like a seasoned pothead, and he takes her hand to lead her to a bench at the foot of the scene.

There's some sloppy, rushed kissing before he hurriedly pulls her shorts off, and her heart is pounding and she can't believe this is happening but she knows for a fact that she is not ready. Not ready for this. He leans her back and stretches her out on the bench. She's flat on her back and he's climbing on top of her. She wants him to look at her face but she can't—doesn't know how to—tell him to look. At her. *Can you see I don't think I want this?* She watches his face as his eyes roll around haphazardly in his skull, the whole side of him glowing red from the candles in their votives, as if he were being burned alive from a distance.

He's gone. He's elsewhere. *Take me away, take me with you,* she had wanted to say earlier. But now she sees that he was never *here* to begin with. *There was no* him *to take me along.*

She turns her eyes to the sky, the stars hanging up there, the moon yawning down at her.

This can't be pleasure, she thinks.

Open the floodgates.

She doesn't know how to talk about it, even now. How whiny, how weak, how pathetic, how ungrateful, how clueless and stupid will she sound? *What if you don't even know what rape is and is not? What if you have good reason to believe that the beautiful boy by the shrine is the best you will ever do? Is it wrong to try to find pleasure there?*

TWENTY

Bite your tongue. Close your mouth.

Is it true that Claire has never avoided relationships with women? Is she a sister to anyone other than the person who came from the same womb? *No.* She hasn't given it much thought, but it's true; *I am not really a friend to other women.*

Rebecca is here to help her, to sustain her, and Claire wants nothing more than to tell her to fuck off—to spit in the face of this earnest courier of hope. She shops with Rebecca, pushing the cart down the endless aisles of canned goods and gleaming waxy produce, but she wants to throw the smartly-wrapped crackers and chips and candies at her friend. She wants to step on the rows of bioengineered bananas until their insides smoosh out and coat the linoleum. She wants to shame and embarrass them both. *I want to have it out.*

They make chit-chat. They do the appropriately casual shit-shooting. Rebecca is careful to steer the conversation far away from John. Maybe she can sense that the ground they're treading is laced with explosive devices and that Claire doesn't need much of an excuse to trip one.

There's such a thing as a violent smile. Spend enough time with women who've agreed that they ought to hate each other and you'll see it right away, the smile that says I'll kill you. Divide and conquer. Room for one or none at the top. Watch your back. And god help you if you're fat.

Claire's good at it, though she'd like to believe she's not. She has lots of practice. She can scan the others and calculate their social currency in split seconds. *Women are just too smart to make for good friends,* John had once said to her. Sometimes it played in her mind on a loop. *What the fuck does that mean?*

———

Claire knew nothing of all this as a child. She was as naïve as they come, thinking people either liked other people or they didn't, simple as that. Early adolescence was rough for her. She was not practiced at narrowing her eyes in assessment and intimidation. She didn't know that wearing the same pants as one of the cooler girls could get you in social trouble. She had no idea that being intentionally ignored could feel worse than being called a dumb slut. Girls and women make excellent functionaries of the state when they commit the minor violences that boys can't be bothered with.

But oh the poor boys. They didn't really have it much easier. Or did they?

By the time she noticed that they had different social rules than the girls, she was already at the end of middle school. She admired their cool, their freedom (or so it seemed to her) to proclaim their love for whatever band they wanted. They could be cutely disheveled, look a handsome mess. They got to be the scholars, the star athletes, the artists, the lead singers. Even the quiet ones could be unhurriedly, interestingly brooding. Not so for the girls.

Claire and Rebecca maneuver their bursting cart around a mother and her two young children. The little boy is riding in the cart. The little girl is standing beside her mother, whining gently about something the mother has said. Claire feels a stabbing sadness when she looks into the girl's eyes.

Are you smart? You look like you could be. Keep your head down.

The world will forever underestimate and ignore you, until the day you discover your sexual authority and use it, despite your hunch that you were noticeable—noteworthy—all along. Keep your backpack on. Keep walking. The teachers—even and especially the women—will ignore you too. Just get used to it.

(Daisy Buchanan should have wished for her daughter to be a loud and sexy beautiful fool, not just a beautiful fool. It takes sexiness, loudness, brashness—suggestively stealing many spotlights from many boys—to make it in this world.)

Whence this bitterness? This anger? Was it new? *Nah. Just always simmering.* A slow, gentle simmer. A low enough heat to ignore, most of the time. But not all the time.

All those boys on their skateboards, edging into the street. Those boys with all their audacity. Those boys who in their (her) youth had seemed so dangerous, so interesting, so set on flirting with every kind of counter-cultural stance, so *curious* and even so worldly, had all turned out to be content to be nothing more than proud vegetarians who still listened to NOFX or Weezer, ethical commitments fixed, living in mid-size houses in the sprawling developments on the outskirts of town with their unthreateningly pretty and put-together wives. A sea of women who spend their days in Lycra, making healthy meals to eat with their husbands and children. Juicing to the tune of Richard Hell. Yoga with The Pixies on in the background. Comfortably oblivious to the forces that were shaping their lives. Not worrying that the air conditioning now needed to run year-round. *They* had food and water and shelter; how could it possibly matter that so many others didn't?

When she had first encountered the boys, as little more than a girl, she had felt deeply inferior to them. Unno-ticed by them, she could watch them as they skated past her downtown, spitting on the sidewalk, their hair proudly in their faces, their bodies made thin from their political veganism. She could watch them as they sat around and read their Vonnegut, talked about the Zapatistas, cursed the mind-control tactics of television and religion and school. She imagined they would all travel the world, write their novels, make their music, paint their anti-authoritarian murals on the sides of buildings in urban centers—convince the world to fall in love with them.

When she sees them now, as an adult returned to this small town, she wonders if they would ever suspect that they were part of what drove her to leave that town, to do her best—in her twenties, at least, *before I sunk*—to make the world fall in love with her.

All these years she thought she was *catching up* to these incredible boys and their otherworldly girlfriends. But now she sees that she mistook all their actions—their adolescent poses—for fundamental commitments to living in a particular way.

The naiveté some of us never push past: she didn't know back then that ideology could be fashion. She didn't know that ideology won't live your life on your behalf. *I have been living like the rest of them,* she sees. *I am no different than them.*

It can't be this way any longer.

She thinks of that little girl, whining next to her mother, in front of the frozen waffles. She wants to travel through time, wants to go find herself at that age, tell her that for a long time she won't be okay but that she eventually will, even if for a moment. *Sometimes a moment is enough.* She wants to tell herself not to be afraid.

Is there anything other than submission or suicide?

Rebecca pays for the groceries at the check-out—sweetly insisting on it—and she gives Claire's hand a little squeeze. Claire's eyes fill with tears and she looks at Rebecca, unsure of how to reveal her gratitude without revealing everything else—everything that Rebecca can't help her make sense of.

She sees that there's something she once knew but had let herself forget: *I can build myself.*

TWENTY-ONE

It's dusk and she is back at the house, putting away the meals she and Rebecca have made. There are two soups and a big lasagna. Family foods. *John loved lasagna.*

Her phone is suddenly buzzing with texts from Luke, saying that he's going to stop by on his way out of town. He'll be there shortly.

He arrives and knocks on the door with a look of urgency in his eyes.

"Let's go," he says. "I have to get back to work tomorrow, I have to pick up the kids later in the week, but you can come with me. There's no reason you can't. You can stay with me for as long as you want. Let's just go." She feels the heat pushing into the house. She knows she should close the door.

His car is parked right outside the house. The street-lights click on. The automatic timers on the neighbors' outdoor lights click on. The crickets have started their symphonies. *Is the dog still out there?*

She looks into his face, his beautiful, earnest face. She wonders what hers looks like just then. Her eyes settle on his. *I have always wanted your eyes to flash at me, telling me that we share some unspeakable secret.*

They exchange a long look. There's excitement and some sadness in it. She feels helpless. *There's an important shared history here,* she realizes. *Is this love?*

I want to go with him. No, I don't know if I want to go with him.

She has to tend to John's parents; she's ignored them for longer than she ought to have. She has all those meals in the freezer. She has a mountain of letters and emails and cards to respond to. What keeps her from getting in that car with him and going? Going and going and going?

It's not duty. Not devotion to John. At least she doesn't think so. It's not propriety. She's not worried about what the neighbors will think. It's not even sadness.

No, it's fear. Fear that she is always wrong, always mistaken, always in possession of the bad idea. The deepest fear, the one that feeds all the others, is that she's nothing more than a fool and a loser, worth nothing to everyone.

It doesn't matter that Luke is standing in front of her saying that she matters to him.

She glimpses a life of riding in the car next to Luke, the sun and wind in their hair. Perpetual escape. Escaping life for the rest of their lives. They smile knowingly at each other. They pull over and make love in the backseat. They are always sweaty, but they don't mind the heat. They spend afternoons lying naked on blankets in the dirt. She feeds Luke bread, he brings her wineglass to her lips. They read novels aloud to each other, sit in silence for hours together, stop whatever they're doing to watch a murmuration of starlings sweep across the sky. They escape to the furthest edges of the desert and they never look back, building a gorgeous glass cube of a house, cacti and bougainvillea and birds everywhere, friends always visiting and wine always flowing. And fresh food: warm baguettes and ripe peaches. Somehow, there is water all over the place—pools, lagoons, lakes—and shade.

All they have to do is look at each other closely—being as still as possible—and their entire souls will be visible to each other. They're Charles and Ray Eames, only more attractive, more arresting. They're Verlaine and Rimbaud, without the murder. They're Joan Didion and John Dunne, but unknown and utterly indifferent to recognition. They're Patti Smith and Robert Mapplethorpe, only less poor, somehow. They're everyone at James Baldwin's colony of the stateless in Saint-Paul-de-Vence. They are all other beautiful losers —lost, exiled, and happily so. In the middle of nowhere, ready for death, for sudden vanishing, on everlasting honeymoon.

She knows how much of a fantasy this life is. *I wouldn't even know what to do with so much beauty.*

She wipes it away and returns to the fear. The fear is one of her best friends. She has always known it. But for good reason, really. She isn't a fool for listening to the fear, despite the fact that the fear is *of* being a fool.

She has always known that eventually the party ends. Everyone goes home and you're alone with a mess. When you really need the help—when you're desperate for anyone—there's no one.

There is no such thing as help.

She could drive to the ends of the earth with Luke and she might still be alone.

They don't really say goodbye, she and Luke. She tells him as best she can that she needs time, which is true, despite how much she also wants a warm body—his warm body. They share a sad, lingering hug—*a lonely hug,* she thinks—and then he rushes off. She watches him open his car door and climb in. *What if I never see him again either?* Her heart sinks. Will she ever go with him? Will she ever plummet again? She can't know. He can't know. There's something she can't give in to just now.

She wants multiple lives running at once—three or more distinct ribbons of time intertwined so that she can run away forever with Luke, grieve John and be fair and true to him, return to her former self and erase her mistakes, erase her acts of self-erasure, become a mother and understand what it is to live for someone else. *Must female subjectivity be split into a thousand pieces?*

What she wants is to live as though life doesn't demand an impossible unity of us. *Another fantasy.*

She climbs the stairs to the bedroom and closes the door,

something she rarely does. She sits at the edge of the bed and stares into the wall. *There are small nail holes there.*

She is waiting for something. *John.* Someone.

She stares at her palms, twists her wedding ring.

You will never leave me, she thinks to him, as though he could hear her thoughts. *Are you comforted by that?*

She wishes she could dream about him. She wishes she could somehow put her sleeping self to work figuring out how to carry on after him. *So many things I long to tell you. So much I need to say.*

She wishes someone could tell her what to do.

She will eventually go to sleep tonight, she knows, and she urges herself to do something with that sleep. *Please come find me. Please.*

TWENTY-TWO

In the morning she walks downtown, hoping the rain comes again while she's out.

She has no umbrella. She's wearing a thin white dress like Simone in *Story of the Eye*.

Will today be the day the world burns down? Will a wildfire sweep across the landscape and consume everyone? Will the torrential rains fall and fall and wash them all away?

Let it happen, if it's going to happen. This is worth something, she had once thought.

She feels strange, as though she is only partially weighed down by absence. She has something like a spring in her step, despite getting only a few hours of sleep after Luke's departure. She can feel the strain behind her eyes that accumulates when sleep is absent for too long, but no matter.

She's a mirage out here in the desert, a dream, just spun sugar and blood.

She's waiting in line at the café, suddenly hungry and thirsty. She knows Andrew often comes here to write and read; since she and John moved here she's avoided this place because of it. Because she hasn't wanted to be caught one-on-one with Andrew, to be subject to his intensity, to sit at a table with him, knees touching underneath.

There are two people ahead of her in line, a young couple that seems vaguely familiar to her. They see Andrew enter the café and take his place at the end of the line.

"Hey, you remember that guy?" one is saying to the other, with a chin tilt toward Andrew. "There's only a couple ways a guy like that is still alive. Either he's still in and out of rehab—long enough to give his system some kinda break every once in a while, or he's found Jesus. He found Jesus and got clean, I bet."

She turns around to see Andrew; she knows it's him they're talking about.

She's wondered herself if he would have a Clean Period as a True Believer. *He's not clean, he hasn't found Jesus. He's just another shitty guy. The world is for him and no one else.*

Andrew sees her, moves to join her in line. He slides up next to her, snaking his arm possessively around her waist. She turns her body to his and gives him a friendly side-hug, pretending to be oblivious to the way his arm skimmed the middle of her. He gives a slight nod, as if he understands what she's doing, as if he knows that it's important to her to keep up appearances.

They haven't spoken or seen each other since the other day, the morning in the diner. *I'm not sure I care if I ever see him again.*

"How are you?" he says with his mouth close to her ear. The couple in front of them turns around quickly enough to catch a glimpse of the scene, but not long enough to gawk.

"I'm alright," she says. "Just in need of coffee and breakfast."

"Can I join you?" he says loudly enough for the gawkers to hear, emphasizing that this wasn't a planned rendezvous. For all they know, Claire's virtue may still be intact. It's Andrew's version of a nice gesture. He normally couldn't be bothered to do any kind of appearance-upkeep.

They spend a moment or two at the table, drinking their coffee. She likes looking at his shoulders. She likes the way he holds his coffee cup even when he's not drinking from it. She has no desire to talk to him.

Ready. They both know what's coming next.

She stands up and begins walking toward the back of the café, where there are two spacious bathrooms. She turns around, knowing she'll see him following her.

They lock the door behind them and tear their clothing off as though it's on fire. Andrew forces his fingers into her and her breath catches. She bites his ear so hard it draws blood. She has teeth and she can bare them. He slaps her face away in a small reflexive movement. They fuck quickly against the wall, her legs wrapped tightly around him. It's uncomfortable, awkward. Her back scrapes the wall where shit particles land as the toilet flushes.

She wishes she had her period. She wants him to have to watch as she bleeds.

After Andrew is finished he drops to his knees and takes as much of her in his mouth as he can, saying he needs to taste her, he wants to eat her whole. *This will be goodbye,* she thinks. *Don't come back.*

She weeps as it finally ends. She is tired. There is no surrender into a sea of sweeping desire for her. Not now. The libido keeps an untidy ledger.

She is learning to let herself go. *It is not a simple pleasure.*

*Don't come back to yourself. Don't come back to yourself.
Don't come back to yourself.*

TWENTY-THREE

That night she wakes from a dream in which John was stitching her mouth shut. *If you're a woman built by a man, does that make you part man?*

He had a thick needle and thin string, he was bent over her sleeping face, and he was working quickly so as not to wake her.

She jolts from the dream to a hazy moment. She knows she is awake, but reality is shifty, unclear. She takes in the darkened room around her, feels the squishy give of the blanket covering her legs, and she doesn't need to put her hand to her mouth; she knows John has not been sewing her mouth closed.

She wishes she could open a window.

She's awake now, as she has been most nights since John's death. Alone in the dark with whatever she can bring herself to think or feel.

Every night is different.

Sometimes she sees him, she can stand to remember conversations, she lets herself think about him, she has the strength to miss him. Other times she can't do it— she needs distraction or else her heart will drop down to her knees or escape her body altogether. *You can wake up now,* she'll have to tell herself.

On the day he died, there was a moment when she got the call, after she hung up, still in something like disbelief, that she felt a little release. Like something that had been stitched to one of her ribs was cut loose, snipped off by a surgeon digging in her chest. It almost felt like relief.

But now she knows that it was the beginning of a kind of destruction. Destruction of herself, her life, everything she had come to rely on to make her *her.*

Let's have steaks for dinner.

Had either of us said I love you as he walked out the door? Is 'dinner' the last word I heard him utter?

If our lives are houses made of lies—ten thousand little ones and a few really big ones—her house just couldn't stand anymore. Now she can see it: something elemental was cut loose.

It was her ability to do all the lying that building requires. To be a social creature, to be Aristotle's little political animal, to be responsible to others, as she always had been. The sorrow would soon overwhelm her and drag her to the bottom of its pit, but at that first moment: a tiny release. The beginning of undoing.

I want you to undo me.

So now: cut loose. Unconfined. *Undone.*

No more smiles for strangers. No more polite nods and concerned yes-I'm-listening head-tilts.

And no more of that worst lie of all, the permeating self-deception womanhood had required of her: *I'm fine, thanks for asking.* It had been her refrain, her mantra for her entire adult life. Always fine.

But now. She would have no choice but to let herself crumble. It lands with sorrow: *I will have to be what I want.*

Her foundation was too shaky anyhow. Her baseboards had been coming up for years. Or she could burn herself down, if she wanted to.

John was not here to stop her, to tell her what to do, to reach out for her, to say *The things you do matter.*

Will he undo me forever? Or am I the one doing it now?

Why bother? Why bother with anything? Because, she knows, *we ache with unfulfillable wants.* We are feverish with desire to be more than we are. Because we can't stop hoping that our chunks of bone and blood and flesh can somehow exceed their casing, that we matter, that these desires that make us shake with fury are indicative of more than a biological imperative to reproduce. *It's the wanting to carry on that is the exceeding.*

It is about love. It is about beauty. It is impossible to really live if it is not about these essentials. Love and beauty are not truth. Neither implies goodness or virtue. Neither is always pleasurable. Neither is always worth it. But both will change you, if you let them. They will require co-becoming with whomever or whatever brought them to you. This is what she now knows. *Love is never far from fear.*

Or we do stop hoping, we do give up. *Yes, some of us stop hoping. And then we kill ourselves. Quickly or slowly, it doesn't much matter. Submission and suicide are the same thing.*

We wander into the River Ouse with stones in our pockets if we're ready or we live half-lives of action at a distance, knowing flesh and blood are too messy, too precarious, that they guarantee pain, that it's easiest to just do what we're told. *If you've still got some light in you, then go before it's gone.* This is also what she knows.

What I know. But she has no idea what to do with it. Not yet.

Is this grieving? she wonders.

It's still the middle of the night, and sleep is nowhere in sight. It's the opposite of when she was a child and being awake at night, alone, always frightened her.

Tonight the night is fine. It welcomes her sorrow, her fear, the dread that lingers everywhere in her body, and it offers no advice, no judgments, no concern. Tonight the darkness is her only confidant.

But the sun comes up. *The goddamn sun just keeps coming up.*

TWENTY-FOUR

She sees the sky out there, past her window, past the houses and the buildings that surround hers. It's a landscape that shows off—that *flaunts*, with malice—how the sky stretches for forever in every direction.

This is a place where the sky and the land are so striking they play a kind of character in her life—a place where she must confront them both, everyday.

She is exposed here, exposed to everything above and below her. If she stays out long enough here, she'll die. The earth will suck the water from her. The wildlife will make quick work of the rest of her. A leash-less dog, going from nowhere to nowhere.

The openness, the vastness of everything around her slams into her even on a drive to the grocery store. When she stops at the Shell station for gas. It's the most punishing beauty. It's pure possibility.

She tries to imagine conducting the rest of her life here.

She tries to imagine making sense of, or giving two shits about human lives or *a human life* or anything here, in this place that is only ever a reminder that she too will end, and maybe should never have been.

She touches her face. *I am here nonetheless.*

ACKNOWLEDGMENTS

Thank you to the readers of shitty first drafts: Randy Sproat, thank you for the Penélopê insight. Thank you for the years of precious friendship. You have always been the total artist. Laura Cline, thank you for using your sharpest knives on this text in its early stages. Thank you for honest and kind encouragement--the most generous gift a friend can give. Michael Sloan Richards, thank you for your unconditional support and for the epistolary relationship of a lifetime that has nudged this book along on more than one occasion.

Thank you to Leza and Christoph and everyone at CLASH, for believing in this book, for taking big risks, for caring, for bringing new possibilities (literary and otherwise) into being.

Thank you to the members of the Detroit City Seminar. Thank you for the reminder that community is what the artist seeks, even if it is a community to come that the artist herself may never live to see. This reminder came at a crucial moment in the life of this book.

Thank you to the friends and family members and strangers who offered encouragement in all its forms. You have sustained me.

Thank you to Philippe Best. For everything we have been and will continue becoming, I hope to have the strength and patience to give you what you have given me: "I don't need to see your artwork, because I see you living." Thank you for how you live. Thank you for living with me.

Thank you to the readers of this book. Thank you for reading.

ABOUT THE AUTHOR

Lindsay Lerman holds a PhD in Philosophy from the University of Guelph in Ontario, Canada. She works as a translator and teacher. This is her first novel. She lives in the U.S. Follow her on Twitter @lindsaylerman

Photo by Sandy Swagger Jones

Big Bruiser Dope Boy

TRY NOT TO THINK BAD THOUGHTS

Art by Matthew Revert

SEQUELLAND

Jay Slayton-Joslin

JAH HILLS

Unathi Slasha

GIMME THE LOOT: STORIES INSPIRED BY NOTORIOUS B.I.G

Edited by Gabino Iglesias

NEW VERONIA

M.S. Coe

THE HAUNTING OF THE PARANORMAL ROMANCE AWARDS

Christoph Paul & Mandy De Sandra

DARK MOONS RISING IN A STARLESS NIGHT

Mame Bougouma Diene

TRASH PANDA

Leza Cantoral

GODLESS HEATHENS: CONVERSATIONS WITH ATHEISTS

Edited by Andrew J. Rausch

CPSIA information can be obtained
at www.ICGtesting.com
Printed in the USA
LVHW090916210919
631814LV00002B/24/P